THE LAST GRASP

Jim Webster

THE LAST GRASP

A Tale About a Medical Octopus

ISBN #:   Softcover   0-7388-3486-6
Library of Congress #:   00-192616

This book was printed in the United States of America.

To order additional copies of this book, contact:
Xlibris Corporation
1-888-7-XLIBRIS
www.Xlibris.com
Orders@Xlibris.com

CONTENTS

DEDICATION

For my wife, who over the past 50 or so years has been my constant source of inspiration. She has not only tolerated but often encouraged me in my foolish attacks on windmills and all my many other absurdities.

PROLOGUE

In the first third of the twentieth century, medical care in the United States was inexpensive and generally ineffective. Cures came infrequently and were usually the result of surgery for such straight-forward threats as acute appendicitis or cancers. Other common killers, such as heart disease, high blood pressure, and stroke were typically not considered to be curable and quite often not even treatable. Although romance and drama were always associated with medicine, through the 1930s it was a classic cottage trade, with thousands of small hospitals and physicians who toiled independently in relative isolation. It involved only a small portion of the United States economy. In those days the big money was in manufacturing automobiles or in oil and in real estate investments.

After World War II, however, there was a dramatic transformation in American medicine. It entered a truly scientific era with impressive rapid gains in the effectiveness of new treatments, so that cures or the promise of cures became commonplace. Concurrently it became a huge industry, primarily as a result of massive government financing, embodied in such initiatives as the National Institutes of

Health for Research support and other federal programs which generously backed the financing of hospital construction, medical school development and emerging technology. The total volume of government and private dollars designated for health-care rose spectacularly, as new discoveries and therapies came into common use in hospitals, clinics, and even in physicians offices.

As the volume of money funneled into health care increased exponentially, a new group of professionals was attracted to the field. These were not M.Ds or Ph.Ds, but were entrepreneurs who recognized that health care delivery was evolving into an enormous segment of the economy, and was readily accessible as an investment opportunity. They appreciated that if they could apply commercial principles and the industrial model to medicine, while leveraging their capital through stock offerings, unparalleled possibilities for profit were theirs for the taking. Best of all, they were working in an environment of trusting patients, unallied doctors and inefficient hospitals, absolutely vulnerable, defenseless against an organized assault using conventional business oriented strategies.

As a result of all these factors, medical care has become the fastest growing segment of the American economy in the past twenty-five years. It employs one of every eleven working Americans, involves over a trillion dollars a year, and accounts for more than one-sixth of the Gross National Product of the country. The fictional tale that follows takes place during these, the most tumultuous times in the history of American medicine.

CHAPTER 1

Scott Richards stood motionless looking out of the enormous picture windows in his private office, contemplating the Little Rock sunset. It had been an early spring and the hills had already turned a rich, brilliant green. The executive suite was set into the peak of the pyramid that crowned his TransNational Healthcare tower. He especially liked the totally glassed-in effect of this open space atop the pyramid, since he could see in every direction, and savor the breadth of the landscape that the hundred-and-ten-story, ultra-modern headquarters building commanded. His office was elegant without being ostentatious. The motif of marble and steel suited him just fine. He also liked the fact that several layers of security had to be negotiated to get to him, unless you had a smart card for the private elevator . . . and there were only six of those. At first, he'd not been so sure that the pyramid set exactly the right theme, but now he rather fancied that too. The architects had been persuasive about "pyramid power" and besides, once he'd approved the design and decided where it should be built, he had other much more important things to be concerned about. He let others deal with the operational details.

He resumed walking after this brief moment of thought. He considered final details for the upcoming annual stockholders' meeting of TransNational, two days away in New York. He already knew how he was going to report on the details of the "merger" with American Healthcare, his fourth largest competitor, and hopefully a second deal that would allow him to complete his stranglehold on the medical marketplace.

His private line rang and he walked to his imposing glass and chrome desk and picked up the receiver. He was disappointed when it turned out not to be the call he was expecting. Instead it was Joe Thomas, the Chief Counsel of TransNational, and he sounded shaken. "Franklin's dead," he said. "Suicide." He was talking about Associate Counsel Ken Franklin, who had been in charge of the American/TransNational Healthcare merger and who had just ended his life by putting a bullet into his right temple. The Little Rock police had already ruled it a suicide and the local newspapers were on the scene.

Scott slipped into his high-backed leather swivel chair, put his feet up on the desk and took a deep breath. "Damn! Dumb, dumb, dumb," Richards said. "All he had to do was keep it to himself and not be so goddamn sensitive. You've got to keep better control of your people." Yet Richard's mind was already working. "Well, let's get two releases going," he said. "The first should be an official one stressing the tragedy, 'A valued colleague will be sorely missed' and so on and so on. Then, leak the second one. Imply drugs, personal issues, sexual problems, whatever. Reflect on anything except what he was doing with the merger. Tell all our new *partners* that this changes nothing, except that we need to be absolutely certain about security. Thank god he wasn't on the stockholders' meeting program. Call me if there are any problems, but just do it."

After he hung up, Richards thought how glad he was to have done this sort of thing before, so that he knew how to handle these problems. Nothing could be allowed to interfere with the events which would unfold in the next few days. The meeting in New York would be the crowning achievement of everything he'd planned over the past fifteen years, completing his control of American health care.

His brow furrowed as he scrolled through the meeting agenda on his computer. making a few changes. then rose again and looked west into the fading profiles of the low back-lit hills. His eyes rested on the TransNational Healthcare corporate logo which was engraved into the windows and the embroidered curtains. It was a dogwood flower superimposed on a physician's caduceus. and it drew him to thinking of his Little Rock roots. in the city where he'd now become successful beyond even his wildest ambitions.

His thoughts were interrupted when his private line rang again. He hoped that this was the call he had been waiting for. It was. George Whitney. the head of security for TransNational. sounded excited which for him was most unusual. He was calling from New York where the stock market had been closed for a few hours and tomorrow's financial strategies were being settled.

"Well. you've done it." he said. "Occidental Healthcare is obliterated." Scott Richard smiled. "They'll never be able to meet their dollar obligations. Our man there has just faxed me their confidential closing profit-and-loss statement. and since you've blocked access to the kind of new capital they need. they've got to come to you. They'll fall right in your lap. I expect they'll call you tonight . . . and checkmate! You're a genius." Richards smiled again. "With the announcement of the American Healthcare merger in two days and the Occidental acquisition." Whitney went on. "the market is basically all yours. Great timing!"

Richard's smile was unchanged.

"Do you think you'll get into anti-trust difficulties?" George was good at espionage. but always two or three steps behind in tactical planning.

"No. don't let that worry you. I'll deal with it." Scott had already prepared the ground for that. In over 400 cities across America. TransNational had a reputation for propping up hospitals and doctors to keep them financially solvent. Now he'd be able to call the tune for both of these former major competitors. to set the payments to the clinics and the physicians. cherry picking whatever hospitals he wanted to include. "Thanks George." Richards said. "See you at

THE LAST GRASP 13

the meeting. Bring all that stuff with you—; no point in taking any chances sending it."

He sat back thinking about the annual meeting and the next two days. There he'd announce the deals: The capture of American Healthcare, and now Occidental as well. Of course, they would be called mergers, but he'd prevailed. TransNational would get control of all the assets. These two takeovers would effectively make him King of the medical industry, with much more than half of all the health resources in the country under his personal direct domination. Ten percent of the Gross National Product of the United States would be his to command. Once again, he smiled his tight-lipped grin.

As darkness completely filled the sky, he went back to his plans for the annual meeting, but reminiscences kept intruding.

CHAPTER 2

Twenty-five years earlier, Scott Richards had arrived in New York City, which had presented an awesome sight to him, since at that point, he'd never been farther from Little Rock than Memphis and the beaches of Panama City, Florida. His arrival in Manhattan at the West Side bus terminal gave him a realistically bleak perspective as he surveyed the other newly arrived travelers, the bag people, the young addicts and miscellaneous street people. He was impressed that the few employees at the bus terminal at that time of the morning were impassive and uncaring. They were obviously used to such problems. Missing at this time of day, of course, were the pimps. They knew that late afternoons or early evenings were the most productive hours. He looked around and then with a concentrated effort to appear confident, ascended the stairs. *So those are the rules here,* he thought to himself.

In truth, he was well prepared for such an environment. In the beginning there had been real childhood deprivation. His father, a graduate of the University of Arkansas Law School, had undertaken a career in personal injury law and found that baby Scott's arrival had significantly interfered with his life plans. Shortly thereafter, he had informed Scott's mother that he no longer wished to be married and doubted that she would get much of a settlement since he had already planted groundwork that would demonstrate she was an unfit mother and that unless she accepted the pittance that he was planning to send her each month, she would find herself in even more desperate straits. She had been trained as a primary school teacher, in the best Southern tradition, and her own mother had always preached that passivity was generally the best course of action in dealing with men, so she placidly agreed to his terms and the marriage was terminated, although in truth, her parenting had always been exemplary. Actually, Scott's father's behavior was not unusual given the family background and traditions. His great-great-grandfather was a cavalry officer acclaimed for his organizational skills and aggressive style. He had been killed in Chicamagua. His grandfather had been involved in bootlegging and moonshining but was pardoned as a result of local political intervention, and eventually became sheriff of a small county in southern Arkansas where organized crime had flourished during prohibition. Scott had continued in the family tradition of opportunism, working in high school as a messenger where he watched and learned as his employer, the Little Rock branch of a corporate New York law firm, racked up huge profits manipulating the system and the clients it was allegedly serving. They specialized in mergers and acquisitions and his preference was to frequent the employees' cramped lunch area. He found this an especially advantageous educational environment to learn about the behaviors, culture, attitudes and tactics of a sophisticated, smoothly functioning law practice. In his last year of high school, as a result of counseling from a college advisor, he had been able to find an obscure scholarship for Sons of the Confederacy who demonstrated academic promise and had managed to enroll at a prestigious university in New York City. He intuitively knew that the credentials of an Ivy League diploma was what he would need to launch his life successfully on its yet unformed pathway.

His arrival later that morning at the University was another completely new experience. Registration was being held in a characterless building that was replete with pseudo-gothic trimmings which looked to Scott to be covered with the dust of the ages. The diversity of the freshman class was something which he hadn't anticipated. Graduates of the prep schools, all of whom seemed to know each other, or at least could identify each other as peers, were congregated in one area. The foreign students also networked and animatedly clustered together. Another clearly identifiable group were the self-assured native New Yorkers, who were unfazed, acting bored and annoyed and loudly complaining about having to stand in line while registering. He realized that he was not part of any of these cliques, although it was obvious to him that the preppies were the elite and, were he felt, where he really should be. The question of how to get accepted was a problem that he mused over as he queued up to talk to the Assistant Dean of Students, who was responsible for student employment. Scott's scholarship covered tuition and books, but nothing else.

Dean Berkowitz was clearly an unhappy man, curt and scowling. Having to tolerate a horde of intelligent but unworldly students, so many of whom had not a shred of real-life work skills, and trying to match them to the market was not his idea of academics. "Richards." He looked up at what he perceived to be a corn-pone Baptist. "How about an evening job at the library? That should suit you."

"What's the pay?" came back Richards.

"Minimum wage but you can probably get some studying in and it's easy. You southern boys should like that," he added with a condescending tone.

"I don't want easy. I need the money. Why don't you look at my record, Dean Berkowitz?" he said, matching the Dean's sarcasm.

"Oh, so you want a challenge." The Dean picked up the defiance in Richards' tone, and scanning his résumé said, "Well, in that case, let's see. Since you've had some experience with the legal system, why don't you try this? It's with Hanrahan and Klein; they specialize in accounts collection, especially medical. It's a factoring operation . . . have any idea what that is?"

"Yes." Scott knew from having heard about it in Little Rock at the table where the firm's hired help sat. These were collection agencies that acquired long overdue bills from hospitals and doctors, debts which were considered impossible to collect. The agency worked on a percentage, the older the accounts, the higher the percentage they kept, beginning with fifty percent after three or four months. Most often these were individuals whose initially inadequate insurance coverage had been exhausted and the providers of services—the clinics, hospitals, and doctors—were left with a large unpaid balance. Frequently, the work involved instances where the patient had died and the enterprise had to attempt collection from the next of kin, or estate if there was one.

"It's all commission," the Dean said as he handed the referral slip. "The last four students I sent over didn't last," he threw out with a snarl. "Good luck," was his parting admonition.

Two hours later, after unpacking in his cell-like dorm room, Scott ascended the stairs in the seedy, off Times Square, four-story building which housed the offices of Hanrahan and Klein. It was squeezed in between two much taller office buildings which were equally down at the heel.

"I've been referred from the University," he said to the receptionist who was busy working both her gum and her electric typewriter, at breakneck speed.

"Okay. Sit it. It'll be awhile," she said. No magazines or coffee were offered.

From a door labeled *W. Hanrahan* came an angry one-sided telephone conversation. As Scott had nothing to do but observe, he studied the environment. Off to the right were about ten cubicles, each with a desk and at most of them sat a collection of tense young men and women with headset telephones on. They were alternately looking at monitor screens and stacks of papers while working on keyboards. They all seemed to be constantly straining to finish their conversations. The Hanrahan office became quiet.

"There's the University student applicant for yesterday's spot," he heard the receptionist say. Ten minutes later the door opened.

A middle-aged, somewhat disheveled looking man in a short-sleeved wash-and-wear white shirt motioned Scott into his office with the introductory command of, "Kid." The office contained a worn desk and a battered credenza, which were covered with ledgers and stacks of papers. Two threadbare chairs and a tilting floor lamp completed the décor. The window behind the desk had been rendered opaque due to a layer of dirt which appeared to be approximately of the same age as the building.

"So you think you can collect for us, huh?" he began. "What makes you think that you're man enough? You'll hear every whiny, hard luck story, every lie and evasion in the book. The last three students lasted about two days each."

Scott was aggravated. "You want to know why you and this job don't look so tough to me?" he said. "Okay. I'll tell you. I was born in Little Rock and I always had to fight my way out." And he told him some of the life events that transpired. Starting with his father, his education in the Little Rock Public School system, and his working to help support the family. He left out some of the personal aspects of his early deprivations. For example, following the divorce there was never any attempt at shared custody. His father let it be known that he always had more important things to do than tend to his son. When Scott's mother suggested that perhaps Christmas or another holiday would be appropriate for a paternal visit, these suggestions were met with disdainful remarks of "why spoil a nice day by spending it with your brat." When Scott was eleven years old, a family funeral was the setting for a chance meeting with his father, who on this occasion, along with other pleasantries, assured both mother and son that the monthly child support that he paid was "the most unproductive money he ever spent; and he looked forward to the time when this nose bleed would be stemmed." Scott had gotten the message. When the time came for college, Scott's developing sense of self-respect had caused him to request his mother that she not ask his father for any help. She however took it upon herself to attempt one more time to get some additional financial support and called the senior Richards. She related to him the news of Scott's high performance in the college aptitude tests and told him how the college counselor described Scott as having "terrific potential." His response was a predictable, terse "I never throw good money after bad and your son has about as much potential as a local cow flop which as I think of it would be a good nickname for him, good-bye." Unfortunately Scott heard the details of the conversation third hand, and was appropriately infuriated with both parents. That was the moment when he subconsciously resolved that he would not just survive, but would become pre-eminent in some very visible way, to vindicate and prove to himself and his father, and to the world, that he was truly meritorious.

Hanrahan rewarded him with an amused expression. "Okay, kid, it might work. Check with Maria. Third cubicle to the left. She'll show you what to do."

Maria was less than thrilled. These frequent orientations cut into her opportunity to get her own bonus commissions, but what the hell, he wasn't bad looking and was college. "Here's how you access the accounts on your desk," she pointed out to him as she hooked up the keyboard, which was tied onto to the headset. "Read the scripts, they tell you what you should say depending on the circumstances. These deadbeats have all gotten the form letter in the first packet. Here's what you can't do and say," as she pointed to the yellow sheet hanging next to the screen. "Though if things get hot, we sometimes bend these rules a little. You figure it out. Remember, you only get paid for what you collect. The closeout on each call is coded to the screen when you hang-up. Mr. Hanrahan, by the way, can listen and watch what you're doing and he does. Any questions?"

"Yes," Scott asked. "How much can you make if you hustle?"

"Couple of hundred in a really good week. Night is actually the best time to call. People are home, they're tired and you can really beat 'em down. Anything else?"

"No."

"Well then, I'm going back to work. Good hunting."

Scott scrolled through the accounts. They were indeed residuals of either large doctor or hospital bills, where the health insurance, such as it was, had been collected and the remainder, often thousands of dollars, was being pursued. If the patient had died, the code indicated that you were to go after the next of kin, who were identified. The job actually suited Scott very well: the flexible hours, the opportunities to use his articulate aggressiveness, his insensitivity to personal misfortunes and his willingness to work the fringes of the legal system were all well adapted to a system for bullying the "client." By the time he was a sophomore, he was pulling down more than $1000 a month in commissions. Mr. Hanrahan, who sometimes eavesdropped, caught him crossing the legal borders, but instead of issuing a threat of dismissal, Hanrahan had only given him a mild reprimand and advised him on how to do it better and legally.

As he became comfortable in this occupation, he became very interested in the flow of dollars, although he never really linked them to the tragedies of the people at the opposite end of the conversation. He sometimes entertained himself by sorting them into various categories. Those who hadn't read the fine print of their contracts; those with massive bills that just outran their benefits; those who were simply confused about their rights and options and didn't know how to make an appeal to their insurance company, which he figured was the largest group. There were the true hard luck stories which he personally considered a small minority. It didn't occur to him that each phone contact involved human beings who had been beset in one way or another by catastrophe.

Gradually, as a result of his activities, he realized that the whole payment scheme for medical care was chaotic and insane, all the while appreciating that it was being worked to the advantage of so many within the system, as well as those on the periphery such as Hanrahan and Klein. Slowly, it dawned on him that if he ever had an opportunity to organize the system, it would not only result in significantly more money through increased efficiency, but it could offer huge, untouched revenue sources for whoever could control it. He was intuitively smart enough to see the potential volume of dollars to be gained, even though he couldn't yet integrate the whole picture.

He thought to himself, *somehow there has got to be an opportunity for an organizational masterstroke here. Someday I'd love to find it.*

School was going so well that when he learned the University was offering a new graduate seminar course in the history of health care financing and delivery, he was intrigued. Piqued by his job experience he decided to sit in and audit it. This turned out to be an event that changed his life. The professor was Walter Rand who was visiting on a sabbatical from a California futurist think-tank. His lectures initially focused on the background of how waste and a cost plus mentality had blunted all attempts to make health care economically responsible. All the charges were simply passed on to insurance companies who paid in full without question and then passed the increases on to employers or the government in the form of increased premiums. So, Rand pointed out, it was hardly surprising that the cycle had spiraled up and up and would likely continue to do so. Rand reviewed the alternatives; his solution was to cap costs with a universal government sponsored system. This was the mid-1970's, and such "socialistic medicine" concepts were not, to say the least, mainstream. They were considered poison by the American Medical Association, the American Hospital Association, and the insurance companies who happily added their overhead percentage to every increase. Rand also went into the detailed specifics of medical accounting practices, and some of the very fine points of how things were done and how the system could be transformed.

No student in the classroom paid more rapt attention than Scott Richards, who felt that he had suddenly been shown the Holy Grail, as he furiously scribbled notes, trying to follow the professor's outline, sometimes adding his own observations in the margins. This unified all the pieces he was working with, at Hanrahan and Klein. He was stunned by the total picture, all of the uncoordinated components, all the money surging through this chaotic industry essentially without any central organization. As the educator paced back and forth, railing about the doctors and the hospitals who, in his opinion, were raking in all this wealth taking advantage of the misery of others. Scott was racing ahead thinking of how he could systematize such chaos.

His thoughts were interrupted when Professor Rand said, "Next session I will review the barriers that will likely prevent this from happening in our lifetime." As he usually did at the end of the sessions, Scott bolted from his seat and bombarded the speaker with questions formed during the previous two hours. As the other students left, tiring of the dialogue between the academic and the intense undergraduate, the teacher queried, "Young man, what's your interest in all this? You obviously aren't a bean-counter type."

Scott told him about his job, the specifics of which didn't surprise Rand, but as Scott outlined the dollars, even he was appalled by the scope. "Young man, let's adjourn to the cafeteria so we can talk."

Scott was thrilled. He appreciated that he was going to be getting a tutorial. They slid into a back booth at a nearby bustling coffee house which, in the best New York tradition, was alive with intellectual energy. Scott listened intently as Rand reviewed the medical power structure. "Even though the delivery system was fragmented, the basic organizational apparatus was actually set up to be cohesive, so as to assure maintenance of the status quo," was his consistent theme.

Scott leaned forward and asked, "But if the government can't get control, what's to stop a private entrepreneur from taking over the lion's share?"

Rand laughed. "You mean to corner the medical market? I'll tell you, it's prosperity." Scott looked surprised. "You see," Rand continued, "there's effectively a gentleman's agreement between all the players. No one in the system wants to kill the golden goose. Until the whole process plays out, pricing itself out of the market, it really won't be transformed. Oh, there'll be some fine tuning but no real opportunity to do what needs to be done, which is total restructuring. I figure that the breakpoint will be when the health costs are 15-20% of the Gross National Product."

Scott sat motionless and fascinated, running numbers through his head. At the present, health care was 5-6% of the Gross National

Product and already at $200 billion a year! "You mean $500-600 billion!" he blurted out.

"Well, adding in some general inflation, it would probably be more like $900 billion to a trillion at that point," Rand replied. Scott did some more quick arithmetic.

"That's 3% of the Gross National Product of the whole world," Scott gulped.

"No, closer to 4%," was the reply. Rand lit his pipe. He could see the young man, like himself, was an expansive thinker. But he also sensed that he was not looking at an altruistic human. Correctly, he sensed that Scott's focus was on how to acquire some of this. "You're trying to see how to get a piece of this?" he baited Scott.

"No, I'd like to capture the whole thing."

Rand was appalled by the arrogance of the response. "You're serious, aren't you?" he asked. "Well, young man, if you're serious you are worse than any of the sharks currently in the business. The saving grace is that neither you nor anyone else could do it." Rising from the table, he abruptly strode off, paid his bill and left.

A somewhat chagrined Scott Richards sat towards the back of the room at Rand's final seminar, all the while suppressing a smile. He had a plan, even though it was at this point indefinite and fuzzy. He had already started a reference file on trends in health care organizational funding. His approach was not unlike that of his great-great-grandfather Randolph, who had consumed everything he could about cavalry tactics and organization while a student at West Point. When the war between the states came he went with the South, of course, and his careful studies had allowed him to develop the most highly organized, most aggressive cavalry troop in the entire confederate army. Robert E. Lee had always felt that Randolph's death at Chicamugua had been a turning point for the South. In an army filled with great leaders and horsemen, Lee believed that Randolph had eclipsed even Stewart and Jackson as truly a unique general. Scott's middle name, incidentally, was Randolph.

CHAPTER 3

New York City's social life in the seventies presented itself as a remarkable environment for a work-addicted student from the South.
There always seemed to be something going on and available any-
time, and with a little planning there were numerous opportunities
for casual sex and transient relationships. Given his early life experiences, this was exactly right for Scott. Not that he wasn't interested in
gratifications of the flesh, but his goal was much more oriented to
power than emotional comfort.

His next bed partner in New York, he had decided, was to be
Maria from the Hanrahan sweat shop. She was amused a few nights
later when he suggested that they share dinner. And having been
well-schooled in such things, she was more than ready for a match
since it was quite apparent what he had in mind. After several drinks
when he suggested going to her place, she asked, "Whatever for?"
She was sure that his arrogance and relative lack of worldliness would
allow her to have great fun at his expense. Scott fell right into her
game plan. "How about another drink or two first?" she suggested,
knowing that he'd been up 24 hours straight, and 65 of his last 72.

studying for his final exams and then having to show up for a six hour session at the law firm.

Scott assured her that this idea of another drink or two suited him "Just fine," since like many men, he erroneously believed it would lower her inhibitions and elevate his performance. It was late when they got to her West Side studio apartment and he suddenly felt more tired than he had expected, though not ever "too tired", he thought.

Maria teased, "Let's watch some TV first and I'll slip into something comfortable, kind of like an old married couple. There's beer in the icebox," she added as she stepped giggling into the bathroom.

Scott dropped into a chair and flipped on the TV to Channel 32 where Alec Guinness reruns were holding forth. He tried to get into it but was fading. Sure enough, Maria did reappear having changed into a halter top and a leather skirt. "Okay, lover," she announced on entering the room, "Let's dance! That's how we do it in my world." And with that she switched off the TV and in the same motion started up the salsa records as if she'd done it before. Scott dragged to his feet; this was not exactly what he had in mind. She energetically started to move to the beat and as the velocity of the music increased he tried to emulate her strut or at least to keep up. After several minutes, he retreated to the overstuffed chair.

"Come on!" she taunted. "Let me get you another *cerveza* and then it's off to bed."

"Let's skip the beer," was his retort.

"Okay," she said. "But I'd like to be romanced only with slow moves and soft touches."

Scott was already trying to figure a way out. He was now well aware of his likely inability to perform thanks to the long hours and alcohol. "I think I'm going to be sick!" he blurted out. By this time, it was actually partially true.

"Hey, come on!" she slipped her halter straps halfway down. "I thought you were *macho* and we'd have some real good fun, but well, okay, Romeo, don't try to walk home. Get a cab, it's rough out there at this time of night." Scott retreated rapidly from the field. By this time he knew that Maria knew she'd triumphed. Since she had lots of men in her life, missing a night or two didn't really hurt. As he stumbled down the stairs, she laughed until her sides ached.

The next day, he was not looking forward to seeing Maria at work. Actually, it never came up. She knew the rules and she'd won and there was no need to push it further. As with most of his past and future life experiences, Scott turned this one to his advantage. First, by vowing never again to be maneuvered into such a disadvantaged position. Second, he reminded himself that there were many strong women in the world whose initial perceptions might be deceptive. And finally, for the short term he'd likely do better with "dates" he met in the singles bars. As part of his life plan, he knew that it would be crucial for him to marry well when the time came, but that was still a distant issue. For now there was undergrad school and then law school.

His goal, like most of those in the pre-law classes, was to be accepted into Harvard and judging by his first three years, he had all the skills and could acquire the knowledge without difficulty. There were, of course, the Law School Aptitude Tests, which had to be successfully mastered. Like everyone else he took the local cram course, but he was still worried since he didn't always test well in the multiple choice format used by this examination. One night, a few days before the exam date, he received an interesting call from an ex-high school classmate. "Scott, how are you? Last time I heard, you were hot for law school."

"Yes, Charlie, that's right. What makes you call right now?"

"Well, through a friend, I've come across something that you might find interesting. I might be able to get a copy of the afternoon half of the law aptitude tests and an associate could provide the exam and the answers to you at lunch on the day of the test."

"How much?" Not one to beat about the bush when important things were at issue, Scott demonstrated early the negotiating style which was to become his hallmark.

"$2000."

Scott calculated the four or five weeks it would take him to earn the amount. "$1500," he came back.

THE LAST GRASP **27**

EBS

"You've got a hearing problem? The price is $2000," his ex-classmate replied. Keep jerking me around and it'll go up to $3000. You know we can't do too many of these or the testing group will catch on and the crib sheet won't be of any use to you or anyone."

Two thousand dollars it was and the details were settled. It happened. At lunch, a business colleague of the caller showed up. He looked to be straight out of a B-grade movie about New York City drug dealers. When they were outside the exam site he set up the rules. "You get the exam when I see your money, $2000. I pick up the exam back here at 1:25. No Xeroxing, no sharing; any problems and the testing people get an anonymous phone call about you. Capiche?" They exchanged envelopes and Scott avidly put his mind to the task of making sure he had all the answers in the areas where he was weak. The courier showed up on schedule and Scott went into the afternoon session. He soon came to the appreciation that the $2000 had bought him the real thing and he breezed through the questions. He turned in his paper and went out to celebrate; a most unusual luxury for him.

The next month, there arrived in the mail a form letter from the Law College Aptitude Test. It was tersely worded, the meat of which read, "Enclosed please find a check to the amount of your matriculation fee for the examination given last month. There were some irregularities and a trend of superior performance on the afternoon portion of the exam compared to the morning piece has led us to request that those possibly involved in an irregularity retake the complete exam at no charge next week. We regret the inconvenience that this may cause, but believe that we have no choice." Scott was chilled. The bastards had given out too many exams. God damn Charlie and his scheme. First was the lost $2000, but further he knew that no matter what they said about anonymity, somehow this event would mark him and the schools would know who had been implicated in cheating by having to take this special, out-of-cycle exam. Finally, there was the problem of taking the test itself. He hadn't done all that well in the morning half. As luck would have it he did score well in the "make-up" exam, so there were no further recriminations. He was right, however: the schools all knew, and in spite of his grades and respectable test score, he received what seemed to be a never ending stream of rejection letters that he constantly suspected were because they knew. New York City Law School finally took him, basically because while they probably knew about the special exam as well, they looked at the rest of his record which was outstanding and figured, "Okay, considering our flunk rate, if he doesn't have the goods, he'll be gone by the second semester." They had underestimated Scott.

He knew that to get a good offer from a good firm, he was going to have to be a first rate graduate, since he would come from a second rate law school. He really did feel superior to his fellow students. Many of them were second generation Americans and were scrambling, as was he, but he truly believed his clear WASP perception of superiority. That he had a talent for logic and organization couldn't be denied. Early on, his exams and classroom preparations caught the attention of a number of the faculty. His verbal and written works were constantly well researched and articulate. What was not known and appreciated was the fact that they were the result of 20 hour days as he became one of the most driven in a driven group of overachievers. All the while, he still maintained his working presence at Hanrahan and Klein to fund his continuous preparation for life.

He was doing well academically, always one of the top few in his class, but in his last year he clearly appreciated that he needed something more to catch the attention of his next employer. He had not worked in the Law Review, a traditional pathway for recognition, since his study/work schedule had prevented him from being involved in the politics and the kissing up that he felt was needed to become a senior editor of the Law Review publication. Fortunately there was another vehicle. New York City Law College offered several prizes for essays by seniors. One was in contract law and Scott appreciated the potential that this offered in getting him noticed, especially since mergers and acquisitions were the new New York and Wall Street religion and these required contracts, and this had been something that really interested him anyhow. The project of trying to win this prize soon became all consuming, even cutting into his work at the collection agency which had continued to serve its financial and educational functions well. As his plan evolved it turned out that Hanrahan & Klein was to provide him one last benefit; the focus for his contract essay.

It was so easy. His calls had given him a familiarity with every conceivable patient/hospital/doctor arrangement. He was knowledgeable in all the ambiguities and inconsistencies of health insurance policies. These not only disadvantaged the patients and caregivers to the benefit of the company, but also intimidated and confused the policy holders so that they would not even challenge a bill or contest a cancellation of benefits to which they were entitled. His manuscript title was "The Contemporary Immorality of Health Insurance Contracting Practices." The faculty loved it. It blended a realistic analytical knowledge of the topic with an ethical message which they wanted to market on behalf of New York City Law College and the profession in general. "First prize for the best essay on contract law, unanimously awarded to Scott Richards, who also will receive the School's Oliver Wendall Holmes Award for the outstanding graduate demonstrating innovative legal thought as a student," was the wording of the announcement. The committee was unfortunately unaware that the winner, on a day-to-day basis, had personally used most of the strategies of which he wrote with such contempt, and that he used them to his advantage while collecting commissions from those unfortunate citizens whose accounts had been surrendered to Hanrahan and Klein.

The result could not have been better. Unlike most of his classmates, he had numerous serious job interviews and two offers. He eventually chose to become an associate at McCloud, McGlory and Johnson since they had a basically WASP culture which appealed greatly to him, had branch offices in Memphis and Little Rock and were doing lots of mergers and acquisitions. They weren't doing the huge ones which led to big stock offerings, but the small and medium-sized stuff that offered opportunities for direct involvement by associates of the firm. Situations that offered to contribute to his continuing legal education, working towards his eventual long-term goal, were very important to Scott.

He knew that now was the time to activate a program to promote a perception and presence of social respectability and an aura of responsibility which would befit a member of his new firm. Since his fiasco with Maria, he had indeed enjoyed a number of intermittent transient acquaintances and sexual encounters which left both him and his partners reasonably satisfied. A virtue of such an approach was that when he now wished to come forth and present himself as the son of a socially prominent Little Rock family, it was not difficult. A few introductions and opportunities to escort the daughters of some of the city's leading families came on a regular basis. He was always careful never to take real advantage, to be attentive, and his behavior was amorous enough so that there was no question of his being gay. And never too frequently with the same woman or group.

CHAPTER 4

The law offices of McCloud, McGlory and Johnson occupied three floors of a 50-story mid-Manhattan building. The décor was mahogany, teak and leather. Scott often ironically contrasted his new surroundings with the hardscrabble ambience of Hahnrahan and Klein. With regard to his duties, he found that the work was exactly what he had expected and his life there as a new associate suited him very well. He really did have a talent for contracts and was an apt pupil, as he received instruction from an excellent post-graduate faculty. His primary mentor was Everett McKenzie, a senior partner who, as might be expected from his name, came from a family that had originally settled in Nova Scotia after leaving the warring clans in Scotland. His approach to life and the law embodied the Scottish virtues of honesty, thrift and hard work which Everett considered unalterable cornerstones of success. It was a good fit, when Scott was assigned to be paired with him. Scott had expected fifteen to eighteen hour days and actually found himself enjoying his apprenticeship, and to his wonderment he repeatedly saw that McKenzie actually practiced the high-minded principles that his law professors had previously espoused. For virtually the first time in his life, he had someone he could relate to and accept as a true role model. He was surprised at how important it became to hear McKenzie tell him, "Good job, Scott." Frequently the stern-faced mentor would then, often gruffly but gently, explain how it could've been done even better.

He'd been with the firm about eighteen months when the Harrisburg-Mechanicsport merger came up. McCloud, McGlory & Johnson was representing Mechanicsport Steel who were being acquired by the larger Harrisburg group. One evening as Scott sat scanning his computer screen, reviewing for one last time what was to be the final agreement, which was thought to be ready for signing the next day, he started. *That's wrong,* ran through his mind. He sensed that the leveraged buy-out would significantly be changed by a simple replacement of the word "will" in place of the phrase, "may after mutual agreement" in an obscure paragraph of the document. Presumably this had been done with malice of forethought by the opposing law firm. At once he grasped the significance. Straightening in his chair, he calculated that this would allow Harrisburg to move at least $200 million dollars worth of assets out of Mechanicsport without paying a cent. He was stunned. He realized that even at 1 a.m. McKenzie, who usually retired early, would want to know about this, but damn it, it was his work and his diligence, what if he didn't get credit? He sat paralyzed for minutes until a compromise formed in his head. He thought it was flawless. He would write a dissenting memo, present it to McKenzie in the morning just before the meeting with their names on it as co-authors.

As the legions of lawyers massed for the merger meeting, Scott saw to it that he was among the first to arrive. He took McKenzie aside and made known his findings and carefully produced the solution.

"Hmmm," McKenzie commented as he perused the document. "How long have you known about this problem?"

"Just saw it last night," as he felt the tension rising.

"So why didn't you call then?"

"It was 3 a.m. and you've tutored me so well that I knew just how you'd do it, and by the time you would've got here, it would've been morning anyhow. I'm sorry if you think I screwed up."

McKenzie was pacing back and forth, not a good sign at all. "You know damn good and well how we do things here and this is just not the way we work; you're still an associate, not even a junior partner. However, you are quite right about the problem and it would cost our client lots of money so let's take care of business."

The meeting was a victory, pure and simple. The Harrisburg lawyers retreated in total disarray amid responses of apologies about the "misunderstanding" and "inadvertent error." At the follow-up meeting of McCloud, McGlory & Johnson there were congratulations all around. McKenzie and Scott were heroes, men of the hour and there was no open comment by McKenzie of his disappointment and unhappiness. Scott sensed over the next few weeks, however, that things might never be the same between them, as the taciturn senior partner virtually ignored him.

Three weeks later an event occurred which dramatically changed Scott's life and made the issue of his relationship with his mentor moot. McKenzie sustained a massive stroke which left him paralyzed and unable to speak or write. Even yes or no seemed beyond his abilities. This left the firm with a major problem and Scott awaited the solution with buoyed hopes. At every opportunity he tried to show that he knew all the ins' and outs of McKenzie's clients and their needs. No detail was beyond him, even though this was an especially difficult time for Scott, because his relationships, with his junior associate peer-group, were becoming more and more conflicted. In spite of the fact that most of them were also competing actively in similar ways, they considered him to be especially driven. A constant air of muscular tension was his hallmark. He was six feet, two inches in height at a lean 195 pounds and was always impeccably dressed, often in a new Armani suit. His lean, taut and energetic movements gave him an aura of restrained but unlimited power. All this combined to make him more intimidating than the average lawyer. His behavior, demeanor and appearance were all consistent with a studied impression of a rapidly emerging, successful law career. When he was summoned into the monthly meeting of the senior partners' executive committee, he entered the room with poorly concealed anxiety, a most unusual emotion for him. He hoped it wasn't too apparent.

"Scott," the chairman cleared his throat and paused for emphasis. "We have after some discussion decided to recommend that you be elevated to junior partnership on an accelerated track." Scott felt a surge of exhilaration. "However, as you will be dealing with many of McKenzie's clients who are used to a senior presence, Don Foster will oversee and review your activities and provide whatever guidance he thinks you need. We've done this before in similar circumstances and it's been quite satisfactory. We expect it to work out this time as well. Any questions?"

Scott shook his head. "I would like to thank the committee and let me assure you that I will continue to work to validate this vote of confidence. It will be a pleasure and privilege to work with Mr. Foster." As he left, Scott considered his situation. He did have a leg up on every other associate in the firm, but working with Foster wasn't great.

Donald Foster, Esquire, was a classic patrician, a society lawyer, who had become a problem for the firm. Although his contacts had brought in considerable business in the past, he wasn't suited to their current strategic directions and as he became less involved, his chronic unhappiness and his drinking had increased. Working with him would not be easy. Scott found he really did miss McKenzie and his occasionally paternalistic approach. However, Scott had never been one to dwell in the past and he wasn't about to start now; he'd just do whatever he had to do.

His new status also triggered his next strategic move: a wife and home. He was by now well ensconced in upper (not quite the highest) level, young New York society circles, and he was considered a very eligible bachelor and a good husband prospect. Unexpectedly, Foster in one of their weekly meetings proved to be a matchmaker. "Scott, I want you to do a small favor for me. My wife's best friend has a niece who is recovering from an unhappy love affair, or what do you call

THE LAST GRASP

them now, a relationship? In any case, she's moved into town, her parents live in Westchester and they really are very nice, very wealthy, and socially prominent, but are concerned about her. Money doesn't buy your children happiness as far as I know. Her name is Anne Winter."

"I'm sure it will be a pleasure to show her around, Don." He was obviously not all that enthused, although because of the possible contacts the credentials sounded interesting. Actually, it was far better than he expected. She was not unattractive, perhaps slightly on the plain side, but her features were well put together and her total appearance came off rather well. Her social behaviors were perfect, and her recent disappointment of the heart had left her very, very needy. Scott found her responsive and she was frankly intrigued by his Southern upbringing as well as his comportment of aggressive assurance. His studied confidence and his well developed commanding persona were characteristics lacking in most of the aristocratic and stuffy young men with weak chins that her parents had always favored. The courtship was a New York City classic. Upper East Side restaurants and even an occasional carriage ride in Central Park. When he was with Anne, Scott actually did appreciate that he was somehow a better person and could even comfortably verbalize some of the sensitive and gentler aspects that his mother had tried so hard to introduce into his character. As he analyzed his emotions, he realized that such feelings often made him vaguely uneasy, probably because they conflicted and counterbalanced the raw opposing passions and wounds left by his father's dismissal of him. With Anne, he knew he was, however, different. She embodied a number of the virtues and talents that Scott now realized were very important. Graciousness, tact, sophistication and a light touch were the characteristics that he knew he lacked and these aspects of her demeanor plus her charm and intelligence gave them a very complimentary relationship. For the first time in his life, Scott felt towards a woman warmth, affection and an attraction that was not simple lust. It, of course, was impossible for two such seemingly different temperaments and identities not to have differences. One such spat began with a discussion of how much personal responsibility should a down and out vagrant, who'd approached them for a handout, assume. Following their heated argument Scott realized that in her own very different, gentle but firm way, Anne had a strength of character that nearly matched his own. What rather annoyed him was that after coming to such an appreciation, he respected her for it.

He also appreciated that her world of Lincoln Center concerts and operas gave him a dimension that he had not previously achieved and he perceived that this type of veneer would likely be important to him. He also liked the civility of their association, something he intuitively knew had been lacking in his personal and emotional life as he had been striving relentlessly to excel in his profession. For all these reasons, it was not surprising that Scott proposed marriage to Anne one Saturday night as they sat in her Washington Heights apartment watching the city lights across the way. Her response was a quiet "yes, I think that's a very good idea for both of us."

Her parents had come to respect Scott for his obvious attentions to their daughter and her father's inquires about Scott had resulted in glowing reports about his zealous intensity, his personal performance and his future potential to realize his ambitions.

"Better than the last one," was Mrs. Winter's assessment after their first meeting.

"Something more than he seems, but just not quite right," Mr. Winter had said on the occasion. In any case, when they all met to discuss the wedding, all seemed tranquil.

The wedding turned out rather well for all concerned. Scott played the role of the ideal bridegroom to perfection although he had to be careful whom he placed on his invited guest list. There were a few selected colleagues at work, several designated cousins and some well placed New York friends. Maria and Hanrahan were not among the latter group. He brought his mother to New York City and had her outfitted at Escada and coifed at Elizabeth Arden and then gave her the script including admonitions about what not to discuss. She was made to understand that their previous life in Little Rock was a topic not to be introduced or even commented upon. She understood and was frankly awed by her son's ascendancy from their early circumstances. The ceremony itself was spectacularly planned and formally staged to perfection in the local Episcopal Church, followed by an opulent masterpiece of a reception and dinner at the country club. For the obligatory picture taking and for the entire day Anne was the perfect bride, gracious and elegant, and Scott was the perfect groom. A Caribbean honeymoon followed and then there were the concerns of getting back to work for Scott and for Anne, of making their new home. As a result of their combined efforts things dramatically improved for the Richards. Within six months, Scott had brought substantial new business into the firm, thanks in large part to his new father-in-law's contacts. As a wife, Anne, proved to be the ideal choice for a rising young lawyer. Her parties were well orchestrated and she was delighted to be able to show off her breeding and talents and be involved in her husband's life which was a succession of eighteen hour work days. A minor problem was their sex life. Though she acknowledged her limited experience it was somewhat without passion and some of Richards' demands she found perverse. She finally had to deny him the "bondage games" as he referred to them, although she appreciated that this remained at times a contentious issue between them and might portend future problems for them. Scott appreciated the importance of family life to his continued advancement and success, and settled into this current situation with relative equanimity .

CHAPTER 5

His new father-in-law still had an uneasy feeling about him, but had to admit that Scott had not done anything concrete which would sustain his suspicions. One night his son, William Winter III, freshly graduated and home with his new M.B.A. in accounting, inquired during the cocktail hour as to his father's opinion of Scott, who, William the Third had felt, was physically and by personality make-up a very dominant force and, who like his father, intimidated him. They were seated on their suburban patio as the senior Winter responded, "God knows, he works hard, and Don Foster assured me that he isn't womanizing and he's smart and good-looking. While we're talking about it, son, you should know that we're pleased that you'll be starting a job soon, although for the life of me I don't see why you insisted on a Chicago-based firm." The father's constrained body language showed, even more clearly than the annoyance in his tone of voice, his unhappiness. Unfortunately his son couldn't really deal with his father and certainly couldn't say that he had done it to try, once again, to distance himself from his parents.

"Bill" had always felt disadvantaged, although to the outside world he appeared to have had every opportunity in the book. He was unfortunately stiff and pudgy with an acquired façade of indifference and aloofness. Unlike his sister Anne, his overall bearing came off as one of overwhelming dullness. Perhaps it began with the fact that his mother's pregnancy had been a difficult one since she had been nauseated for most of her nine month confinement. This was a fact that she frequently mentioned to both father and son when she felt they needed to be reminded. Being William Winter the Third was a designation he'd always resented and for years he had been trying to drop it and be "Bill." At the local suburban public school, it certainly hadn't helped when his classmates started calling him "Toidy." Perhaps if he had gone to a preparatory school, it would have been at least okay to be William Winter the Third. Perhaps if he had been a more successful athlete, he would have developed a more positive self-image. Unfortunately, his eye-muscle coordination and his physical skills were such that sports were not a realistic avenue for him to follow to achieve success. And then there was still that nickname "Toidy." "Toidy." "Toidy."

And then there was his younger sister, Anne. While Bill had caught all the problems of childhood, Anne had always been the smartest, most social, and most popular girl in her class. She was also the favorite at home, clearly the apple of her father's eye. Her confidence and self-image flourished, because of her record of successes, further fueling his feelings of ineptitude. In multiple ways it was constantly reinforced upon him that his sister had been preferred, or so it seemed to him. The perceptive observer would have noted that the girls he dated in high school and later, frequently bore a striking similarity to his sister, either in their appearance, their mannerisms or both.

Fortunately, as an inhibited and intimidated teenager, he found that he did have considerable talent for mathematics and for the newly developing field of computers. For a solitary and isolated adolescent this was almost perfect salvation, and a discipline in which he could excel and find great personal satisfaction. He intuitively appreciated that this made managing large numbers remarkably simple and provided an orderly system which he found reassuring. The fact that this relatively new technology often made direct, face-to-face communication unnecessary, was an added advantage. When it came time to consider careers, his preference was clear: computers it should be. His father, who considered them to be flash in the pan toys and simply a slightly updated version of pinball, would have none of it. Business school was where his son would enroll. A minor in computers was the only grudging compromise that Bill could wrest from him. Little could he imagine, as he had registered for his first classes, where all this would eventually lead him.

Two months later, the senior Winters left on vacation to Turkey. A personal driver and automobile for a luxury tour had been arranged; however, what was not on the itinerary was an unplanned meeting with a loaded semi-trailer on a mountainous road along the Aegean. The 3 a.m. call to New York reported that the car had fallen over a thousand feet onto the rocks below and that the remains of the car, its driver, and the Winters were mangled almost beyond recognition. Anne and her brother had never felt so alone. Scott, on the other hand, was very much in his element. He took charge. Among his first tasks was threatening and intimidating the Turkish embassy authorities when they tried to block the expeditious return of the bodies to the U.S. He also arranged the memorial service and dealt with other family members and attended to all the legal requirements and the wills. The Winters had not rewritten them after the wedding so Anne and Bill split everything in the estate, which was considerable. Shortly thereafter, the Richards moved to a brownstone in the seventies, just off Park Avenue.

Meanwhile, Scott had continued his strong interest in following trends in the financing of health care, as the proportion of Gross National Product committed to medical care escalated, just as professor Rand had predicted, nearly into double digits. He used McCloud, McGlory & Johnson resources to subscribe to a computer based legal-medical abstract service which kept him well-informed about the specifics of who the big players were, what was transpiring, and where it was happening. He had always remembered the details of his

WEBS

conversations with Rand and it appeared that all of the socialist's predictions and his accelerated timetable were turning out to be absolutely correct. Scott intuitively felt that now was the time he should be trying to get into the field, but it wasn't clear how he could make this happen, since his current firm seemingly had no interest in starting a medical division. Once again, Foster proved to be an unwitting matchmaker. To Scott's delight, their interactions were becoming shorter and less frequent. And as this week's meeting was about to come to a close, Foster leaned forward and confided, "There's a client of mine who needs a lot of attention, and I want you to help. It's really routine but I need some phone respite from this guy. He's a Texan who is well situated, having made a lot of money in oil. Now he isn't moving very many assets around anymore but unfortunately he needs just as much stroking as when we were setting up his big projects. Since I'm not in the office as much as I used to be, and he needs somebody to talk to I'm nominating you. His name's Frank Powell and he's just like all the other guys in Texas who made it in oil. He's got lots of bucks so let's just treat him so he knows that we know it and things will go fine."

The proclamation having been delivered, he abruptly rose and announced that he was off to his club, leaving an annoyed Scott to do the work of the firm, dealing with the details. Frank Powell's first call came 36 hours later. "Son, I heard from Foster that you're going to help make me even richer. I was mighty glad to find out that you were once a neighbor, well almost. Little Rock at least looks to the West and I know that there are a lot of real scoundrels moving money there, some of them even do it honestly I hear tell. Anyhow, I'll be coming up there next week and I want to meet you and maybe we can do a little business and then I want to take you and your wife out on the town Tuesday night."

Scott moaned to himself as he settled in his chair. This meant looking up the entire file, getting familiar with it, and organizing a file of his own; just what he needed! "What a pain. Damn Foster and his laziness and drink." He dialed home, "Anne, what's on for next Tuesday? . . . Yes, yes, that's what I thought . . . Well, it won't be just an intimate party for thirty of our best friends anymore. it'll be thirty-one. A Texas client whom I have never met will be attending. Sounds like a real jerk, but rich, so plan to turn on the charm."

Mr. Powell presented an appearance that was slightly rumpled with an uncombed shock of white hair. He was dressed in classic Texas style, with a string tie, alligator cowboy boots and a ten gallon hat. As they talked, it became clear to Scott that Frank's speech and body language were direct, and as the firm's file indicated, his reputation of being an honest, strong, hard driving but fair businessman was quite correct. His legal questions were mundane and he was actually quite impressed by Scott who exuded his best Southern persona as they sat comfortably in one of the paneled client conference areas. Powell put out his hand. "Partner, I like your style and I really do appreciate your friendliness in taking me home for dinner with your friends tonight. That's a lot more like Texas than New York City. I'll try to demonstrate my appreciation to your little woman, too." With that he vigorously pumped Scott's hand and strode out of the office.

As the hired-for-the-evening butler opened the foyer door into the living room, Powell enthusiastically burst onto the scene. His ebullient deportment was almost a caricature of the rambunctious Texan and his good heartedness did present a somewhat pleasing contrast to the usual uptight corporate guests at the Richards, business-related social events. As he moved through the crowd, extolling the virtues of the newest member of *his* legal team, Anne actually found him somewhat charming and much less of a bore than Scott had led her to expect. She was certainly rapidly becoming tired of the continuing merger and acquisition technicalities that usually dominated most of the dinner party conversations.

During the buffet dinner as Powell stood next to the fireplace resting his plate and wine on the mantle, he explained to his hostess that his county was almost the biggest, and certainly one of the best in Texas. He put forth the concept that since he had made his fortune there that he was really committed to giving things back to the community from which he had come. This was an altruistic approach that she was not used to hearing from her guests, for whom personal inurnment was generally the holy grail. He was nearly the last to leave and as he did so, he reached into his pocket and dropped a small box into Anne's hand. "Just a little hostess gift, ma'am," he explained. "Open it later."

As Anne and Scott were lying in bed, reviewing the party, she was commenting that she really found him an engaging breath of fresh air, when she suddenly sat bolt upright. "Oh my God, the gift." She retrieved it from the pocket of her evening outfit and gasped, "Scott, look!" A sapphire with diamond flankers rested in her hand. "That must be a $10,000 hostess present, maybe more. You said he had money, I guess you were right. And I liked him even before this."

Scott silently thanked Foster as he fell asleep. Little did he know that soon the relationship with Powell would become even more of a success than he ever could hope or imagine, even in his most ambitious dreams.

CHAPTER 6

Dr. Richard White moved confidently through the morning chaos that was the norm in the crowded Metro Hospital Emergency Department. He was tall, angular, dark haired and sharp featured. His easy movements and powerful appearance were still reminiscent of the all conference Big East basketball player he had once been. He was an imposing presence in any group. His straight-forward and direct style had always been a staple of his character, and at Metro he was both respected and admired. As Chief of Medicine, the ER was part of his turf, and he felt quite comfortable in an environment that to outsiders always appeared disorganized and intimidating. He usually liked to start his day by making a quick pass through this entryway to his hospital, since it gave him an overview of the challenges that lay ahead.

As he moved through to the central nursing station and surveyed the patients who lay on their gurneys in various degrees of distress, he spotted Matt Franklin the night Emergency Department Physician Director wearily finishing a cup of coffee. He knew that Matt had probably been in the job too long, he'd put on 15 pounds in the past year and was basically bored since he felt that had seen everything at least once and at this point really just wanted to get the shifts to end so that he could get out of the non-smoking environment of the hospital and have one of his beloved cigars and maybe a Bloody Mary, if the night had been especially tough. The nurses and staff affectionately referred to him as Dr. Matt, since no matter how rough things got his affability never deserted him.

"Hello, Matt," White said, "anything out of the ordinary?"

"Nah. Couple more poor bastards with central nervous system AIDS. Temperatures to 106. No white cells. The knife and gun club gang-bangers showed up as usual. A bunch of other stuff. There is one interesting guy who's been up at one of the fishing camps in the mountains. Huge boil on the middle of his chest, size of a big grapefruit and he seems really toxic. Can't figure out what it is but whatever, he's really sick; he's in cubicle six."

At that point a wide-eyed intern, who, compared to both physicians, seemed to be barely old enough to be a high school graduate, rushed over. "Dr. Franklin, the guy with the chest wall gumba in six just seized and I'm afraid he's going to arrest; the staff needs help."

"Okay, okay," muttered Dr. Matt unenthusiastically. "Come on over, Rich. The house staff says you're so goddamned smart, maybe you can tell us what's with this guy."

The Chief followed as they walked rapidly and entered the treatment area. In the corner of the examination bay the owner of the fishing camp was siting, with a face that reflected both horror and shock. As the two senior physicians entered, the seizure abruptly ended and the patient lay on the cart breathing heavily in a post-ictal stupor. He did indeed have a huge fluctuant, red, elliptical swelling eight inches long and wide and three inches high protruding from where his breastbone ordinarily could have been seen.

White went over to the stunned proprietor of the camp, "How long has he been up there with you?"

"Five days."

"And what kind of fishing?"

"Fly casting in streams, mostly."

"Do you tell your guests to hang up their waders inside out?"

"No, why should we?" the guide asked.

Matt Franklin interrupted. "What the hell is this, White? Are you a roving reporter for *Field and Stream* or are you trying to get free advice on where they're biting?"

"Brown Recluse spider bite," was the laconic reply of the Chief of Medicine. As a transplanted New Englander, he knew a great deal about fishing and the outdoors. "You see," he went on, "the spider took up residence in your patient's waders overnight and when his new home was disturbed the next day, he took it out on this unfortunate angler. Look at the bite mark in the center of the abscess. Classic for the disease, as is the whole picture. Get him some antibiotic coverage and drain that sucker and he'll be a new man by this time tomorrow." He turned to the camp owner. "And that is why you turn the waders inside out at night, my friend, so that you don't pick up any un-invited guests."

"Got to hand it to you, Richard. Maybe you are at least half as smart as the house staff says."

With that benediction following him out the door, Dr. White hurried off to his office where his 7:30 appointment was already waiting. This was a two-man delegation from Southeastern Medical School. He already knew what their mission was. They had been dispatched to entice him to become the new Dean of their institution, which he had visited three times in the past three months. Dr. White felt conflicted about taking on the job which had been offered to him at his last visit. Not that he felt he couldn't do it, because he was confident of his leadership skills and had always confidently believed that he knew how a medical school should be run, but it would mean leaving the patients, especially the poor and disadvantaged group, that came to a place like Metro. Besides that, it would distance him from the daily interactions with students and interns and residents; something he'd always found gratifying. On the other hand, he knew that he didn't want to stick around the same job too long like Matt Franklin had done. It was a little more money, though he didn't doubt he'd earn it.

EBS

He entered his office, where the two visitors waited.

"Good morning, Mary," he greeted his secretary. "Please come in, gentlemen. Sorry to be late but I was just having a little fun in the Emergency Room on my way to work." And with that he ushered them into his somewhat spartan, unadorned and cramped office which was lined with shelves of medical texts and journals and was remarkable for the fact that the desk was basically clear except for the computer and a few mementos.

His first visitor, a distinguished appearing member of the University board of trustees, who looked like the bank president he was, began the dialog. "We are here to find out what it'll take to get you to Southeastern," he said. "We know you are a great clinician, but we think that you can make an even greater impact by looking at a whole educational research and delivery system; you know, shaping Southeastern into a nationally respected institution. We've looked around extensively and you're the man for this job as far as we're concerned. We don't think it's the salary but if a few thousand more would do it, we'll go back and try and get that commitment too."

"No, it's not really that," White said. "It's what I said earlier when I was visiting out there: would I really have a free hand to do what I think should be done to make the place work? For example, can I just start up a program or institute for ethics in medicine without having to go through the whole, huge University bureaucratic labyrinth?"

"Yes, you could. Here it is, and in writing," chimed in the other member of the recruitment delegation, a sharp featured successful real estate developer, also a university trustee, who retrieved an envelope from an inside coat pocket.

"We rather thought that was your major issue so we obtained a letter from the University's Chairman of the Board of Trustees assuring your autonomy. You can carry out any changes you think are in order and this letter documents the sources of money to do it. It's all there." And with that he handed over the five page, single-spaced letter.

White stepped forward and took the letter. He went back to his desk and sat leaning back in his rustic office chair to read it for some time in silence. "Done deal," he finally said. "Tell them I'll start July 1st."

CHAPTER 7

Frank Powell's next visit to Scott Richards and New York came a few weeks later. It began with a phone call. which Richards took on the speaker phone as he stood at his office window observing the frantic pace of another Manhattan rush hour. "It's a tragedy." the voice on the phone proclaimed. "Our hospitals can't compete with the huge complexes in Dallas and Houston. All over Texas. the smaller ones are in trouble. the country folks can't get local. down-home care and attention. It's a damn shame." The tone was two-thirds anger and one-third anxiety. "I've just come from a meeting with our hospital board. The bottom line is going to be a disaster. I'd like to come up with some cash transfusions. of course. and I'll need you to help me move the money. but that's only a temporary fix: what we need is a long-term game plan." Scott was now all attention. "I sure wish your firm was into health care."

"Well." Richards began. "I think perhaps I can help more than you might expect. I do know quite a bit about the business of financing medical care. I know how you feel about your home county and you've obviously been most generous. Why don't you come on up here. Let's make it soon." Scott realized exactly what this might be and, best of all, the opening was being handed to him on a well stocked silver platter. He rocked back and forth in his chair, almost jumping for sheer joy. A spontaneous sort of thing he hadn't done since kindergarten. He looked at his appointment calendar, "How about the day after tomorrow? The Spurs are in town playing the Knicks and we could use the firm's sky box at the Garden." He knew that Powell was a basketball fanatic and that would clinch a visit. "You bring all the information you can about the hospitals that you want to save; you know, annual reports and especially financial statements and we'll just talk."

"Son, you're a lifesaver. I feel better already." The voice sounded relieved and thankful.

That evening and the next day were filled with frantic activities for Scott as he updated his health care file, and profiled Powell's county and its medical demographics. He drove the staff even more ferociously than usual so that when Frank arrived he could present a picture of informed solicitous concern, beginning with expressions of interest and sincere assurances that he would indeed try to help. Everything that Powell told him matched the information that his staff had acquired and actually their information was more complete than the Texan's. Scott, of course, had his plan well in mind, and knew just how to play it. The visit went well. After almost six hours of questions and answers, he stood at the window, put on his most thoughtful face and said, "Let's go to the game while I formulate a plan." Something that he, of course, had already well laid out in his head.

Scott relished the Knicks rugby-style approach to basketball, and he found himself enjoying the first half. During half-time he broadly outlined his strategy for restructuring the system and assured Powell that what was really needed was for him to make a site visit to the county. He explained that while he was almost certain about the significant organizational changes that would be required, he knew that as a team, the two of them could pull it off. "How about both of us going down in the morning in your private plane?" was his suggestion. This was too much for the Texan. The fact that he might indeed have an opportunity to be a rescuer and benefactor of the county health system was better than anything he could imagine. It seemed perfect to him and that distorted his usually clear judgment and vision. Scott knew that it was perfect too, but for a very different reason. They both fell asleep that night with great hopes for the future but with expectations that were very different and very divergent.

*   *   *

Scott was sitting bolt upright in the backseat of Powell's limousine as it raced across the flat, dry Texas plains, carrying him between the three facilities that served the health needs of the residents of his client's county. He was furiously writing notes to himself on his legal pad as he outlined his plan. Two of the facilities were outmoded physical plants with chaotic organizational structures, ill-equipped to meet the needs of delivering medical care in an efficient, modern, cost effective way. Outdated facilities and overgrown staffs with too many middle managers was Scott's epitaph for them. The third setting was a new regional hospital that actually had reasonably good facilities. The immediate problem was that like the other two it had very low occupancy rates, generally running with only 25-30% of the beds being filled at any one time. Many of the patients they *did* have, made for undesirable reimbursement because of their poor insurance coverage, too many were on public aid to suit Scott but he kept this observation to himself. Most of the really good paying "business" was being siphoned off to larger hospitals in Dallas/Fort Worth, Houston, Austin and San Antonio.

Scott shrewdly realized that he needed publicly to come across as a low-key-consultant/fact-finder, with the credibility of being brought in by Frank Powell, rather than as a hot-shot-New-York-lawyer, lording it over these proud Texans by explaining how they did it in the Big Apple. He always arrived in his shirt sleeves without a tie and showed tremendous interest in the physical plant, the patient care aspects, and all the operational issues of each of the facilities. He was always careful to casually mention the need for organizational information; the annual reports, budget projections, any strategic plans and especially the current profit and loss statements. He was secretly delighted and exhilarated by the general lack of business sophistication that he found and at times felt that it was almost too perfect. As a result of his early experience in the medical collection business and his extensive comprehensive files on the funding aspects of medical care, his knowledge base turned out to be just right. He had simply been waiting for the right time to apply these talents, and it appeared the time had come. While others in his firm had gone to legal seminars on the fine points of corporate mergers and acquisitions, he had taken advantage of seminars at Wharton and Kellogg business schools which focused on predicting future trends that were emerging in the medical care industry. When asked why he was so interested in such a peripheral area, he had routinely demurred, "Just for a change." Now he had the perfect laboratory to test his knowledge and skills. His strategy was simple. A consolidation of the hospitals by mergers, which was something God knows he knew how to do, would provide the economies and efficiencies of scale to allow all three institutions to stay in business, although in very different "product lines." Powell's finances would be the glue to make it all happen, and if the hospitals could really be focused and specialized it could happen in a relatively short period of time. Once he had the major assets consolidated in the regional hospital facility, one of the others could be closed or converted to a long-term care, rehabilitation, and nursing home type facility while the other could be converted to an outpatient, ambulatory hospital, which, given the trends in Medicare funding, would probably be a big money maker. Powell, of course, was delighted when Scott gave him a sanitized version of the plan.

Scott planned to go on leave of absence from the firm and when quizzed gave the explanation, "to help a friend and to do something significant in my life." Anne had balked at the idea, "Live there? Are you crazy, I like Frank Powell . . . but not that much." For the first time in their marriage she really asserted herself; Scott had figured she might and didn't really care at this point. Ultimately he knew that she would agree as long as they kept the New York City apartment and she could commute. His partners at the law firm, some of whom were happy to see him go, wondered what he really was up to. Ultimately, however, it was a mutually agreeable parting, and Scott Richards moved on to his own destiny.

He energetically spent his usual eighteen-twenty hour days standing at seemingly endless numbers of podiums, presiding over meetings, reassuring all whom he met and expressing boundless confidence. His presentations to the hospital constituencies of physicians, nurses and staff, the community at large, and to the various hospital boards were long on pledges, although if carefully and critically evaluated, somewhat short on specifics. He was talking about the strategic plan to set up committees and task forces, all the while assessing local talent; measuring who could be used for what, who could be ignored, and who should be terminated. He knew that the one thing he needed was a knowledgeable and hyper-competent financial person whom he could rely on.

Ruth Bonner was the assistant comptroller at Hills Hospital and he found her sophistication and persona quite out of the usual, local mold, which indeed it was. As a college senior she had worked out a deal with her divorced father so that she could go to Harvard business school and complete a Master's degree in accounting. While in High School, she had watched her mother become emotionally reduced to rubble by the divorce and vowed that her life would be such that she never had to depend on anyone for anything, particularly not on a man. Although she had to agree to come back to Texas as part of the deal with her father, she certainly did not intend to stay. She was blond, short animated, brisk and statuesque. Her movements often seemed studied to affect a bearing mature beyond her years. "A Dallas Cowboy cheerleader in a business suit with brains," was how one of her colleagues once described her.

Her first meeting with Scott was at the helicopter pad outside Hills Regional Hospital, where she greeted him. It seemed that they understood each other perfectly from the first handshake. Initially, she warily described the financial details of her hospital

EBS

and demonstrated her in-depth knowledge of the other two facilities as well. Scott appreciated her talent immediately and within one-half hour he used his portable phone to cancel his next two appointments. They talked and he questioned her as she incisively provided more and more details, fleshing out the information that Scott had already obtained on his own and from others. His instincts already told him that this woman was to be his chief financial officer.

That evening he had an obligatory community square dance to attend, but before leaving, he set up a meeting for the next day. "We need to make concrete plans to continue tomorrow at six," was his parting remark. She did not disappoint. She brought in a well-developed local business plan which actually had features that had even gone beyond his initial thoughts. By midnight, the fiscal direction of County Health Network was set. After a per-functory dinner delivered by room service, it seemed quite logical that they would end up in the same bed although it was not at all clear who was seducing whom and who had the most energy to expend. What was remarkable was that the whole episode seemed strangely without passion, for both parties.

CHAPTER 8

Scott knew that what he was doing was going to be a protracted, totally consuming task. He never doubted however, that he was up to it and that he could and would do whatever was required to assure success of this venture, although there were still some ancillary problems to be considered. With respect to their marriage, Anne had chosen to keep New York City as the base of her activities and life. She had rapidly become firmly established as an active participant in multiple charitable endeavors ranging from the junior board of directors of the Metropolitan Museum of Art to being a trustee of a Harlem-based shelter for abused women. She found, somewhat to her surprise and delight, that she was very effective and that her approaches to problem solving were considered sophisticated, creative, and practical and were most often rapidly enacted by her peers. This revelation encouraged her to pursue significant public visibility which gave her great personal satisfaction. To a degree, it compensated for the long absences of her husband, and in truth her fortnightly weekend visits to Texas were generally pleasant enough. She did enjoy seeing Frank Powell, whom she had come to appreciate and admire for his generous spirit and altruistic good-hearted behaviors. Although Scott seemed totally absorbed in his work, she felt that at this point, their marriage was at least no worse than that of many of her peers who basically endured similar separations while residing on Long Island or in New Jersey as their husbands spent twelve to fourteen hour days in Manhattan at corporate headquarters or on Wall Street.

Except for a five day vacation on Harbor Island in the Bahamas, Scott's year in Texas had been an intense, exhausting, exhilarating ride. Now he felt he'd done it. He'd accomplished almost everything he'd planned. Predictably, he was already looking forward to the future.

"Well, Frank, thanks to you, it's really come to pass," Scott remarked as they stood on the speaker's stand which had been erected on the front lawn of the newly designated Plains Regional Medical Center. This was the site of the celebration marking the one year anniversary of County Health Network. "It couldn't have happened without you and your vision."

"And my checkbook," Powell realistically added. It had not been quite as painless financially or personally as he had hoped it would be. He kept receiving negative reports on some of his protégé's fiscal and management methods.

"All true," Richards responded, "but who else could have done it and long-term, the amount of capital that you'll get back should already be close to what you originally invested, maybe even a better return than what the market would have given you." Scott squinted into the bright Texas sun and surveyed the crowd. The administrative staff from the three merged hospitals were there, at least those who had survived the relentless cuts; less than half of the original number. A few nurses and doctors had showed up and some of the local political leaders were there because Frank Powell had asked them to come. Ruth Bonner was at Scott's side. Her tightly cropped blond hair was back lit, glowing as the wind fluffed it into a halo.

The reorganization had proceeded just as Scott had planned. Plains General Hospital, now known as Plains Regional Hospital, had been cut to one-half of its previous bed capacity with resultant reductions in staff at all levels, professional and non-professional. Criteria for decisions on who was to be retained were made on the basis of cost. "Our posture is that a nurse is a nurse," Scott had told the human resources department. "Some just cost more than others." When the question of special training for special skills was raised, he indicated that local in-service educational sessions should be more than sufficient to "retrofit" these interchangeable human resource pieces. He reminded them that overall there should be a local nursing surplus since there were a number of nurses available as a result of similar downsizing which was taking place at the affiliated County Health Network institutions: Central Texas Hospital, now known as Central Texas Long-Term Care and Rehabilitation Center and the former Riverside Hospital which was now Riverside Ambulatory Health Center. Therefore there should be no real problems recruiting nurses at the new lower pay levels. In truth, the Central Texas Long-Term Care and Rehabilitation Center functioned like a nursing home, with patients housed at lower costs. Patients were usually transferred there at the time that no further bills could be sent to Medicare for their traditional hospitalization at the Regional Hospital. Medicare did, however, pay for rehabilitation at Central. The Riverside Facility was where outpatient care took place, much of it in-and-out day surgical services for patients who received bone and joint or cataract operations, which were extremely well reimbursed by insurance companies, or plastic surgery procedures which were paid for in cash. Many of the previously duplicated services at the three hospitals had been eliminated. No matter how it had been accomplished, financial efficiency was being very well served.

Following another one of their customary midnight episodes of lovemaking at Ruth's new well furnished apartment, Scott sat propped up on a pillow with a Lone Star beer in his hand and in an uncharacteristic, unguarded moment mused. "What we're doing here is just applying the industrial model to health care. It's like making widgets, you know. It's just easier here because there isn't any competition. These idiots have been sitting on a gold mine bigger than anything they could imagine, better than any of their oil deals, and since they were doing all right, they never really pushed to do better. Well, you know, as the saying goes, they ain't seen nothing yet." With that pronouncement he finished off his beer, rolled over and began his usual four hours of sleep.

That, of course, was not the speech he gave when he spoke to the faithful at the celebration for The County Health Network. There he stood tall and talked of quality care, new standards of service, bringing high technology health care to the region, and of the shining new era in health care. As he stood behind the sunlit podium in tailored pin-stripes and cowboy boots, he sounded and looked like the new era health care leader he wished to become.

The year had made him truly fit the part. He knew that since 70% of hospital costs were personnel, the way to cut costs was to cut personnel, but unlike the competition he had done the cutting with the finesse of a two-edged broad axe. When the Vice-President for Operations had refused to carry out a particularly egregious order, one that terminated the entire social work department at Riverside, he was immediately escorted by security from the premises and told that the personal effects from his desk would be delivered to his home later that day. As Scott frequently explained to recalcitrants, "we run this place by the golden rule." As long as he had Frank Powell's checkbook, he knew he had the gold and he would definitely rule. Of course, the former Vice-President for Operations was one of the many ex-employees who did not attend the one-year celebration. He was out of town on a job interview, anyhow.

To increase revenues—his other major strategy—Scott early in the course of his tenure, had mandated a review of the likely profitability of various disease categories and their treatments and applied this information to the county health system. His research had confirmed what he had intuitively known: that major cash surpluses were most easily found in common but complex medical areas such as cardiology and cancer, where expensive drugs and surgical treatments could sustain charges that were swallowed without question by insurance companies who, as Rand had pointed out years earlier, just added in their overhead percentage and passed the charges along to employers or whoever was paying the bill. These were called "centers of strategic focus" and Scott developed new programs to increase the volume of care in these areas. Some of them required recruitment of new medical staff who quickly grew loyal to Richards and his efforts, since they benefited from the increased business that accrued. Not all of the medical staff members, however, were quite so enchanted by the changes. A delegation of the old guard physicians from the recently consolidated system had visited Scott in his comfortable, wood-paneled executive office.

"Yes, gentlemen?" he said, opening the meeting. "To what do I owe the honor of such a prestigious set of visitors?"

"We are Texans," said Dr. Stan Wright, previous Chief of Staff and the acknowledged leader and conscience of the group. "So let me be up front. We don't like the direction in which Plains General Hospital is heading."

"Plains Regional Medical Center," Scott corrected him.

"We don't like the fact that dollars are now the primary criteria for everything that's done around here. Before you hoodwinked Frank Powell, this place had a heart. We took care of people first and then asked if they could pay. Now it's just the opposite. In the old days we served the community, rich and poor, the hispanics and the black population as well as the entitled. Now we know that any patients who aren't employed and don't have insurance are referred by the emergency department to the county hospital two counties over. We don't like this and are here to insist that you change the philosophy and the culture that you've installed here. We want the old hospital back." There were solemn nods of agreement from the other three physicians.

"Gentlemen." Scott rose to his feet. "Am I to understand that you don't like the new business that the new programs bring to physicians? Do you have such short memories that you don't recall that eighteen months ago, all your institutions were on the verge of bankruptcy? Are you aware that over half of the visits now come from other surrounding counties?" Leaning forward and rising over all four of his visitors he concluded, "Through our expansion, we are now the biggest employer in the county and you say we're not responsive? I couldn't disagree more. I've saved your collective asses."

"That's your answer then? No change?"

In a deliberate and clipped manner Scott replied, "The change will be more of the same. Good day, gentlemen." The statement came as a challenge.

"We'll see you at the Annual Board of Trustees Meeting, then Mr. Richards, the members of that group may feel differently," and with that the delegation retreated from the field.

Unfortunately for Dr. Wright and his colleagues, the County Health Network Board, which was heavily populated with local business and political leaders, had been well-primed by Scott and Ruth. Scott never went into any confrontational environment without doing his homework. The board members received with enthusiasm the annual accounting statement showing that the fund balance *surplus* was now over twenty-five million, almost more than the entire budget of all the three institutions three years ago. They also liked the fact that this money had been invested in their banks and businesses and that after an initial downsizing of the original labor force of Community Health Network, the new programs had meant jobs and prosperity for the county. Even though these new jobs came at relatively low pay scales, it still contributed to a local affluence from which they all benefited mightily.

Many of the medical staff were also solid supporters of the new order and said so at the meeting. They vociferously disagreed with the old guard who had confronted Scott. They did indeed like the medical boom that Community Health Network had spawned for their activities. The patients they now saw were virtually all employed and had insurance and the public aid and uninsured migrants could jolly well go to the county hospital or to the public health clinic in the next county. What did those people contribute, anyhow? In short, the meeting was a ringing endorsement of Scott and his policy of "supporting the community by building health care," which was Community Health Network's new slogan.

There were a few dissenters. The local bishop raised the question of how to meet the needs of the poor and homeless who were in his flock. Scott had smoothly assured him. "We have a task force studying that question and I do want you to know that it worries me too." Dr. Wright had tried to bring his concerns to a motion. He was shouted down by the other physician members of the board and the meeting adjourned to the parking lot where a real Texas barbecue capped off the day's celebration.

CHAPTER 9

A few days later a caller who identified himself to Scott as the Executive Vice-President of a Dallas business consortium proposed that Scott visit their group at a pending meeting. Thanks to Ruth, Scott knew that this was a collection of the richest of the rich of Dallas who tried to maintain a low profile while leveraging their investments. A majority of them had originally made their money in oil and their currently diversified average net worth made his current backer, Frank, look like a poor relation. The other members were mostly investment bankers, many of whom had ties to Little Rock and off shore banks as well. This was the big league, the really big money players of the Southwest. Scott had to admit that he was fascinated by the prospect of having a chance to interface with these multibillionaires.

"What's the agenda?" he asked his caller, as he settled his new lizard cowboy boots on his desk.

"We'd just like to hear your thoughts on the subject of health care financing and perhaps get you to expand on some of your current activities."

"Hmmm, should I bring any data?" Scott queried.

"No, nothing formal. This should just be an informal chance for us all to get acquainted."

Two weeks later, as he ascended a broad marble staircase opening into a pair of large bronze in-laid doors, Scott had the distinct feeling that he was at an initiation ceremony to a very small and very elite fraternity. The building was a classic chrome, glass and steel Dallas skyscraper. The office was on the 37th floor. To get this far he had to pass through two security checks, not that it was that obvious, but even *he* felt somewhat awestruck by the physical setting which, of course, was exactly the emotion that this environment was aiming to effect. The mood was maintained as he was ushered into the conference room by a well-dressed 25-year-old woman who was wearing at least $10,000 of signature jewelry to compliment her Chanel outfit. As the chairman of the group, who was seated at the far end of the table, motioned him into a chair he assured Scott that he was most welcome and introduced the other fifteen attendees. He then rose and an electric motor soundlessly opened a curtain revealing a back lit projection screen. As he moved to stand next to the screen Scott appreciated that they were projecting a display of the financial progress of Community Health Network.

"Richards, we're impressed by what you've done with Frank Powell's very small nest egg. You took a group of dead hospitals and turned them around and gave him back his investment and even made him a happy man in the bargain. He's always been into that community thing." The latter comment was delivered almost as a reproach. "We also certainly admired the way you did it, the tight organizational approach you used and the business like way you dealt with the initial cost-cutting that was required. We'd like to hear what you'd do if you suddenly find yourself with real investment capital to put into a medical system."

Scott was taken aback. So this was an informal chance to get acquainted, eh? Well he was up for the contest. He grasped at once the opportunity and challenge that he had been dealt and accepted both with enthusiasm. Any feelings of intimidation soon dissipated. He rose to his feet and with his usual confrontational body language began by using the chairman's first name the way no one, who had been newly introduced, ever did, "Chuck thank you, I'd love to do just that." For the next forty-five minutes, he extemporaneously reviewed the rise to world dominance of American health care. How this was due primarily to the large volume of successful scientific endeavors, and how paradoxically the results of this advanced knowledge were still delivered in a fragmented and inefficient manner by a system that hadn't changed significantly since before the second World War. He highlighted examples of duplication and overlapping services, before finally cataloguing a list of ways to take advantage of the fat that had accumulated within the system. He then discussed how to maximize profits, reducing costs by cutting non-technical staff and restructuring contracts for patient benefits, and increasing revenues by utilizing high reimbursement lines of business and opening health boutiques that collected up-front cash for fertility programs, varicose vein clinics, plastic surgeries and so forth. After this, he launched into what he knew they really wanted to hear about—returns on investment.

"Is there some way I can show you some numbers?" he asked. The screen smoothly slid out of the way replaced by a white wipeboard with a full supply of markers. He rapidly demonstrated how a hundred million invested to replicate Community Health Network should give annual returns of more than 50% after two years. He then concluded, "As all of you know, the problem with non-profits, of course, is that all the surplus has to be, in one way or another, or one time or an other, put back into the operation. Therefore, what I am proposing includes making this a for-profit, closed corporation. Subsequently, there would be the option of going public with stock offerings at a time advantageous to the original investors. Setting aside some of the operations' profits into a not-for-profit medical foundation is, often, a surprisingly good strategy since regulations governing medical facilities use of surplus capital are much less stringent than they are in other industries." Scott paused for a moment as he surveyed the group of entrepreneurs, all of whom had obviously been rapt in their attention and now were silently reviewing both his numbers and his message. He decided it was time for the close. "Gentlemen, let me assure you that I've studied the market in great detail, and I estimate that in Texas alone there are at least twenty-two opportunities to replicate the Community Health Network experience without having to go to any significant risk. Thank you for the invitation. Any questions?"

The chairman rose and thanked Scott and suggested that he should make himself comfortable in the reception area and that the group would join him for some sociability as soon as they'd finished some minor housekeeping business. As he left the room, Scott felt the presence of an abundance of stored energy: a feeling that continued to be with him as he passed along the wall of floor to ceiling windows in the anteroom which overlooked the Dallas skyline just starting to come alive with night lights reflecting in the twilight. He knew that they'd be critiquing his presentation and pitch. He was quite right.

"Well boys, what do you think?" Chuck Bell queried the group.

"He figured out what we wanted to hear, a typical smart, arrogant New Yorker. I vote that we go with it, remembering to put him in his place somewhere down the road," said one of the club members.

Samuel Thomas, who at six foot five and two-hundred twenty pounds presented a classic Big-D image, continued, "Chuck, I agree that we should go with him but putting him down may be more difficult than you anticipate. Also, arrogant New Yorker is a redundancy; George, how many times do I have to correct your grammar?" he drawled.

"Okay, anyone else?" Chuck was getting impatient. "If not, I'll lay the deal on him." Scott was brought back into the room. "Mr. Richards." Bell was now standing over Scott and put on his most commanding demeanor, a look he cultivated during his tour of duty in Korea as a Marine Infantry Captain. "We are prepared to offer to make available to you up to one hundred million dollars of unencumbered investment cash, *if* you can come up with a specific, detailed, business plan to demonstrate that the concepts you outlined have substance in reality. Mr. Sloan, the group Executive Vice-President, will be your contact and can go over any details with you. How soon can you have something for us?"

THE LAST GRASP

"Sounds interesting. Twenty days or less." Scott appreciated that his veracity was being questioned by the emphasis given to the *if* and also that he was having to deal with the hired help, even though Sloan had the title of Executive Vice-President. Well, that was all right. What he wanted right now was investment capital, not social rank. "Now, gentlemen, if you'll excuse me, I'll skip the social hour. I want to get back to work." He could play their game too.

Both Scott and the Dallas business consortium believed they'd had a good day. As the group reviewed his response, they were pleased because it appeared this would indeed be a very profitable new business direction for their investments and it appeared eminently feasible. That evening, they all thought that the Glen Livet and the Dom Perignon tasted especially sweet.

CHAPTER 10

As Scott rode the Community Health Network medical helicopter over the barren Texas landscape back to Plains, he was furiously constructing and sequencing a list of tasks to be done using his newly acquired laptop computer. Scott had no doubts he could orchestrate the type of health-care network that would be needed, now that the financial backing was within his grasp. After all, he'd been working towards this all his life; formalizing it shouldn't be all that hard.

It wasn't. Sloan was amazed at the speed with which Scott produced a completely integrated, complex, and comprehensive plan. It was finished and submitted in seventeen days, not twenty. The Dallas business partnership had indeed been poised for a new project of this magnitude, and it certainly was more sophisticated than any similar plan they had seen before for other ventures. These entrepreneurs were uniformly pleased as they reviewed the vision that was evolving.

During this time, Anne had moved to Texas only after it became clear that her husband really was going to remain in the Southwest. She had promised him that she would participate in his life, as she had in the city, providing the social base that was needed, as long as he agreed that she could take a monthly, one-week trip to New York City, to continue her interests there, since she felt that she was now effectively an expatriate. Scott had grudgingly acquiesced, and Anne was as good as her word. She put on barbecues and overblown rodeo banquets. Her gracious hospitality transplanted well and rang true. She had found that although she could not really make the sort of friends she had enjoyed in New York, she was at least part of his life again. As she settled into their new life, she observed that he seemed even more driven in his work. Their sexual encounters had become even less frequent, something that gave her some pause. She had finally attributed it to the fact that the resuscitation of Community Health Network had truly been an all absorbing task.

Making the transition easier was the fact that Frank Powell continued to be charmed by Anne. "Ma'am, I just can't believe that you're not part Texan," was his compliment at an especially successful social event. As he and Anne stood at the edge of the crowd in the line to pick up their chicken and ribs, he had also confided to her that, although he was most grateful to Scott for what he had done to save the three institutions that now made up Community Health Network, and while the network was now the largest employer in the entire area, he was still troubled.

Anne frowned and asked him, "Why!? What do you mean?"

"Well frankly, it's pretty clear to me," he continued leaning on a decorative railing that was part of the fake horse corral trucked in for the occasion, "that I think that he's much more interested in the industrial and corporate aspects of the operation than the people side of providing a service. I'll bet you didn't know that my father was actually a physician here. Died young of overwork, I guess, but he always maintained that the secret of caring for people medically was to care about people. I've always thought that medical care was a very special, one on one, one at a time interaction. Your husband seems somehow to reduce it to an assembly line process. He actually now talks about things like patient through-put and cases per unit of time. Don't get me wrong, Anne," he continued, looking slightly embarrassed. "I'm glad we did this and he did a great turn-around job but I wish. . . ." His expression looked downcast and his speech trailed off.

"Yes?" responded Anne, looking as if she herself just might be on the verge of tears. "You wish?"

"Well," said Frank, "I hear that he's been approached by the Dallas Business Consortium to do a large offering for them. I hope he won't. Not that Community Health Network can't make it on its own now, but that group is the worst collection of sharks I've ever seen in action in my life. They take no prisoners. They've been successful, God knows, but always to their own advantage and the detriment of everyone else. Their capital resources are limitless. They're tied into Little Rock and New York and off-shore banks. They asked me to join once. Told them I didn't like the smell of their money. I guess they thought that was a compliment; I haven't heard from them since," he concluded. By this time he was standing at rigid attention with his fists clenched. Anne sat motionless; there were real tears now. Scott had told her the night before how they'd likely be moving to Dallas in the near future although he hadn't explained to her why this would take place. Her intuition and instincts now made her aware that this was likely a critical turning point in her life. If Scott took on another strenuous, all-consuming job it would probably be Community Health Network in spades. There would be very little, if anything left for them as a functioning married couple. Perhaps if she could have persuaded him to have children it might have been different.

After a brief but intense period of negotiations, Scott and the Dallas Business Consortium did complete their deal. TransTexas Healthcare was the new corporate entity. They were the sole share-holders and Scott was the President and CEO. Ruth was, of course, CFO. Their non-business evening encounters were less frequent since Anne had moved to Texas but still took place, although it was still unclear who was seducing whom. When Scott occasionally pondered over his choice of Ruth as a paramour, he appreciated that their relationship clearly arose out of several factors. In terms of conve-nience, she had presented herself at the right place and time. He had been striving to achieve success at that point in his career when success was not yet assured, and he needed the release and reinforcement that came from the sexual aspects of their relationship. Besides, she had proven much more adventurous in their love making than Anne had ever been. Moreover in her bold and dynamic approach to problem solving, both personal and in business, she reflected his own intensity and, following their liaisons, this always reinvigorated him. This latter facet of their coupling had become less important, however, as his business ventures became increasingly successful. The missing piece in his consideration of their relationship, and his approach to women in general, was of course the undeniable fact that his behavior was only slightly dissimilar from that of his despised father, who had consistently treated Scott's mother so badly and had uniformly rejected Scott as an extension of his mother. This was the one demon that Scott could not face, much less exorcise, and like many such burdens was a potential future source of serious trouble. The sort of thing that often held the future seeds of destruction for many men.

The County Health Network success story was quite simple to replicate, and Scott continued to find multiple opportunities for acquisition across the state. The only limiting factor was finding and selecting upper level staff: The recruitment ads came across, "If you aren't up to an 80-100 hour workweek, don't apply. Mergers and acquisitions experience is required. Exposure to medical environments desirable. This is an opportunity to be part of an expanding company and a new environment." These notices failed to mention that a killer instinct was one attribute that was carefully sought in all applicants. Drawing on his contacts and the bankroll of the consortium, Scott was pleased at how rapidly he was able to fill the crucial jobs in the organization. The position of Chief Operating Officer was filled by Ronald M. George, a younger and less smooth Scott Richards clone, with quite as keen a nose for figuring deals and appraising opportunities. He was short, muscular, always well tailored with dark curly hair graying at the temples. His quick powerful movements were reminiscent of an NFL halfback searching for running room, as he expended increments of a tremendous fund of kinetic energy. He also brought with him an interesting personal and family background.

Ron George, nee Giorgio, had grown up in Providence, Rhode Island. His father, Gueseppi, was second generation. His grandfather, Mario Giorgio, had gone through Ellis Island, found work on a Portuguese fishing boat and, in the best tradition in 1911, when he acquired sufficient passage fare, had sent for his wife, son, and daughter and resumed family life. Two more children were born in rapid succession, the last being Ron's father, who the proud papa referred to as "numero uno" in honor of his being the biggest and most Italian looking of the children. Gueseppi turned out, unfortunately, not to be the smartest, although his good looks and strength had facilitated his marrying quite well. Ron's mother, Mary, was the high school class valedictorian and was initially delighted with her new extended family and life in post-World-War II Providence. She knew that her husband's job involved laundry services for diapers as well as industrial towels and uniforms. What she only gradually came to understand was that this line of endeavor was an integral part of the Mafia, as the organized crime network cast its ever-increasing shadow over New England. Indeed, her husband Gus was involved primarily in enforcement, protecting his bosses interests in maintaining a monopoly for all the related family businesses in the area. Early in her marriage, she concluded that she should never question the occasional all night absences or the fact that his friends, some of whom appeared to be extremely brutal men, all seemed to be in similar lines of work.

Their son, Ronald Mario Giorgio, soon discerned the realities of street life in Rhode Island. By the time he was in high school, he had figured out how the organizational relationships of the businesses in the area assured that all were under family control. Construction, trucking, restaurants, entertainment, and of course, where his father worked. By this time, his father had been promoted to number two in the franchise. Ron had also figured out how most of the affiliated illegal activities; the drugs, gambling, prostitution and highjacking were controlled. Like his Roman predecessors, Ron had a real talent for organization which was to serve him well. He would have likely gone into a line of work similar to his father's, had not his father become focal point for an internecine war between two capos. After being absent from home and business for more than the usual 24 hours, Gus Giorgio was found in the trunk of a stolen car in a Logan Airport parking lot with two bullets in what was left of his temple. As the Boston Globe reported, "this murder has the appearance of an organized crime related hit." The day after the funeral, Mary Giorgio received an anonymous phone call informing her that she had $250,000 designated for her in a bank in Greenview, in western Massachusetts, and that if she would contact a real estate agent named Robert North in Greenview, he would give her the account number and the keys to her new home. The voice on the phone assured her that all this was free and clear and was being done by her husband's friends and business associates. His final admonition was that they leave at once and change their names. They did both.

The family settled in at their Colonial split level house and eventually the semi-rural existence opened a very different world to Ron for whom the lesson of his father's death would, naturally enough, pervade his entire life. With his penchant for organization and keenly honed instincts for self-preservation, a B.S. in Business from the University of Massachusetts was the logical outlet for him. The question as graduation neared was what type of business should he enter? The University placement office made it easy.

"I don't understand it," his career counselor began. "Why don't any of you guys talk with the health care firms that come through here? It's a new growth area for services and it's almost a vacuum. Their entry level salaries are good, and they're growing like mushrooms. Great experience, rapid promotions, and yet everybody wants to work for a computer company!"

"Give me some real data, like who and how much," Ron said.

"U.S. Medical, for instance, starts at 32K, not bad considering that the economic policies of our President are generally savaging the job market something fierce."

Eventually, Ron ended up going to work with a small California based HMO that allowed him the latitude to learn multiple skills needed for managing, in what was indeed, an expanding industry. At the same time, he acquired formal advanced business training at UCLA at their night MBA program and was informally, on a daily basis, sharpening his already considerable natural talents and hardscrabble skills in contract negotiation. His bosses appreciated that this was something in which he already excelled and they were more than willing to have him take a lead role in dealing with company and union representatives with respect to employee benefits. Similarly, they were repeatedly impressed as they watched him hammer hospitals and clinics into submission. He found the chase and cutting the deal exhilarating, and a natural adaptation to living on the edge was apparently one of the genes his grandfather and father had passed on to him. He was the perfect choice by background, training and temperament to be hired as part of the senior management at TransNational Healthcare.

CHAPTER 11

The TransTexas Healthcare Management was looking for health care institutions that either invited them in or could be easily ensnared. The attack plan used all the skills that Scott had developed in New York City as he watched Michael Milliken and the others devour one company after another. The strategy was simple—you look for hospitals or other health care providers with good tangible assets, for example, endowments, physical plants, and locations, which were burdened by poor management and operational deficits. The only other requirement was that they exist in highly competitive areas with good market opportunities, or places where there was no competition. Scott and company went in as saviors or as bullies, or sometimes as both. His requests to most of the hospitals were simple. In return for providing the necessary operating cash that allowed them to continue in business, he wanted 50% of the Board seats, his own financial officer as second in command, conversion to his software accounting system, at no charge, and a change from a not-for-profit to a profit status. For all of this he gave a generous purchase price to more than pay off any debt. In addition, he offered stock options as virtual bribes to physicians he wished to retain. In reality of course, these changes resulted in Scott's having total operational control of the business. And as soon as one of the Board members converted to Scott's camp, usually after receiving a promise of stock options, Richards controlled policy. The hospital Chief Executives were effectively immobilized, unable to fund their strategic programs unless approved by TransTexas Healthcare, since the newly transplanted Chief Financial Officer would not release the money. Furthermore, since only Scott and his staff understood the new accounting system, all fiscal submissions had to be accepted as being the final, unassailable answer. TransTexas Healthcare, of course, did achieve significant classic economies of scale by mass purchasing equipment, drugs, and services but they never passed along more than a small portion of these savings to the local hospital system. Eventually, the hospital leadership and the community representatives would realize they had made a Faustian deal, but by then, it was irrevocable. Generally, they quietly left, too ashamed and guilty to protest. Occasionally, intimidation and threats of blackmail needed to be employed to ensure there was no unpleasant publicity. Of course, Scott used well conceived public strategies to achieve respectability. He would point out that unlike his not-for-profit competitors, he was contributing to the tax base of the community, though always at a very favorable rate achieved either by using the previous zero basis of the hospital when it was not-for-profit, or by manipulating the local assessors or politicians. Scott also emphasized that they were providing local jobs, though staffing was light by usual industry standards, and less skilled workers were utilized (for example nursing aides to replace nurses) in place of higher level professionals. Eventually he wanted to acquire a medical school and perhaps a linkage with a religious based hospital system. These would come later.

Recruiting for TransTexas Healthcare turned out to be relatively easy and establishing a new culture was something Scott Richards excelled in and enjoyed. He found that there was a large reservoir of competent, talented, and aggressive individuals who, like himself, were just waiting for the opportunity to make money and a name for

THE LAST GRASP   75

themselves . . . and Scott's organization was just the vehicle to empower them. As part of their orientation, they each received a confidential manual which laid out the gospel and commandants according to Richards:

1) Costs of health care for employers and patients had risen 500%, unrestrained for more than thirty years, so there was an incredible opportunity for systems that promised financial efficiency.

2) The relative value of the dollars spent on health care had been decreasing during this same period, fueling employers insistence for change.

3) In view of this, it was inevitable that large organizations should take control of the delivery of care, their scale eclipsing efforts at solo, or small group, doctor practices and small, unaffiliated hospitals.

4) Cost will become the driving factor in deciding where employers and patients will go for care.

5) An evolving competitive model will revolutionize health care, and the winners will be those who are most efficient.

6) TransTexas Healthcare will purchase hospitals and enmesh doctors into our system to control delivery of services.

7) Vertical integration is the strategy, since it will allow us to control all facets of health care, from clinics to hospitals to outpatient surgeries to home health care to nursing homes.

8) Cost control will be our second major strategy as we become the "Wal-Mart" of the industry.

9) Using our size and capital, we will maximize control of all competition.

10) We are destined to become the dominant player with respect to the entire industry.

Scott had carefully thought out the components he would need to effectively manage the corporation he envisioned. His first requirement was the development of an extensive software information system, so he went to Boston, interviewed eleven applicants and finally hired a 28-year-old who once again, like himself, had extremely strong skills and who thought that working a hundred hour week was just part of the job. He also knew that internal security was important, as was "fact-finding," which meant in reality industrial espionage, spying on the competition, obtaining their crucial internal data. To oversee this part of the business, he hired George Whitney, an ex-FBI agent, retired after 25 years of anti-terrorist work. He brought with him contacts with the CIA and a number of other investigative types who worked at the legal margins of the system. He looked a little like a somewhat larger G. Gordon Liddy, a coincidence that Scott rather enjoyed. Even more important for the business was legal counsel. If rapid expansion was to be the order of the day, there couldn't be any lawsuits that might screw up or slow the process. This type of talent Scott knew about.

As he interviewed one candidate with a promising background over lunch in a private conference room at the new, highly functional, contemporary headquarters of TransTexas Healthcare, he outlined the needs. "A foolproof approach is what I'm after," Scott said. "One that safeguards us from antitrust and also ties in anyone affiliated with us in, so they can't escape to compete. We can't be wasting time mobilizing new resources each time somebody waffles." He then went back to his steak tartar. The interviewee made the fatal mistake of saying, "Yes, but . . ." and giving a lawyer-like discourse with a number of "on the other hand . . ." clauses. After hearing the candidate out, Scott addressed the main course and assured the candidate that while he should feel free to finish his dessert and coffee, Scott had to leave due to a pressing engagement.

Then there was the requirement for "techies" to run the computer based information and accounting support systems that were being developed to manage the business. Scott admittedly did not have an in-depth understanding of what was involved in developing the infrastructure for the type of operation he had planned. He knew that he would need detailed financial accounting, a knowledge he did not possess. Nor did the staff he currently employed. One evening in a foul mood following yet another fruitless presentation, he was sharing his problem with Anne as they sat in the backseat of their limousine when she said, "Well, husband, at the risk of interfering, might I suggest you consult Brother Bill? He's just finished a big job for Citibank and is developing one for their Visa affiliate, so someone thinks highly enough of him to commit pots of money, even if you don't think he'll amount to much."

"Well he's not exactly Bill Gates in terms of net worth," Scott retorted as they sat in traffic. He did have to admit, however, that the thought of using his brother-in-law had never really occurred to him. He couldn't be any worse than the crop of losers he'd been seeing recently. "You know my feelings about nepotism," he said after a moment's pause, but the idea was already starting to intrigue Scott, since he felt that Bill would never challenge him, and could be a great spy in the accounting department. It wouldn't be forever and if he couldn't perform he'd be out just like anyone else in the organization. How much harm could he do? He'd find out through some contacts at Citibank Visa in the morning and he'd follow-up. "Well, dear, for you, I'll consider it," was his final response as the limousine slid to a stop at the Four Seasons hotel, where they had an obligatory black tie corporate event.

His meeting a few days later with his brother-in-law took place in the sterile environment of an airline VIP lounge at Kennedy Airport . . . and it seemed even to Scott, rather remarkable. Scott's people intuition made it clear to him that Bill was still quite awestruck with the idea of TransTexas Healthcare and Scott, and that he felt this was a chance to ascend into the big leagues while at the same time, to somehow help take care of his sister since their parents were no longer around. Bill had always seen in Scott what he felt he could never be in terms of Scott's broad reach on problems and planning, his ability to dominate and lead people, and his aggressive, hyper-confident demeanor and style. They quickly settled terms of his responsibilities and an outline of his position. The salary request turned out to be much less than Scott had expected, and substantially less than the demands of other techies whom he'd already rejected. Clearly Bill's enthusiasm for TransTexas Healthcare was showing. When the deal was done Bill rose and with unfeigned emotion shook Scott's hand and said, "It's wonderful to be joining your team at last. I know that this is the best thing that could have ever happened. I'll bust my back to do everything that you want."

"Thank you, Bill. I'm sure it will be mutually beneficial," replied Scott with considerably less enthusiasm. He made certain that it was understood by everyone in the organization that Bill was hired help and not to be treated as "part of the family." Ruth, of course, also appreciated without needing to be told that Bill was not privy to their special relationship which still took place although the liaisons were becoming less frequent. At the end of a tough day or a big project, they still were a satisfactory event, which somehow seemed now more a ritual for release than fired by inspiration.

TransTexas Healthcare, now built in Scott's image, was positioned to burst upon the scene. As might be expected, Scott planned a corporate blitzkrieg. He had teams who were simultaneously targeting multiple hospitals using the criteria he had outlined to the Dallas Business Consortium, and he had carefully chosen each institution on the basis of what he considered to be a constellation of fatal flaws—too much local competition, poor management, a budget shortfall, or weak leadership. His designated teams continually went for the throat with an approach that combined bribery, intimidation, and blackmail. They picked several crippled medical centers for the first phase, to be held as examples for the next round. He taught his minions to use exactly the same tactics with which he had founded County Health Network: approaching everyone working in the local hospital administration, letting them know that if they were "cooperative" they'd be retained and if they weren't TransTexas was going to acquire the hospital anyhow and they'd be out. Pitch to the trustees assuring them that TransTexas only wanted 50% of the Board seats and that the money paid for the assets could be put in a Board determined charitable foundation. The beauty of this ploy, of course, was that as soon as Scott offered stock options in TransTexas Healthcare to the physicians and Board members, he had his captive majority and the foundation dollars could then be short circuited to pay for "charitable" aspects of the hospital operation thus enhancing the TransTexas Healthcare profits. For example, any poor patients who got admitted by "mistake," or any shortfalls on Medicare billing which other hospitals simply considered bad debt and therefore wrote off as not reimbursable, could be paid off under Scott's scheme by transferring foundation money to the operations budget. All of this quite legal as a result of the skillful work of his adept legal staff. The medical staff was offered stock options as bonuses for "efficiencies" for example, for not providing expensive, complicated treatments, except of course those that were well reimbursed. It all worked. The TransTexas teams carried out the takeover details as soon as the contracts were dry. They acted as an imperious army of occupation in well-tailored business suits.

Every Sunday, these organization men and women met in the soaring chrome and glass temple that served as the central corporate office of the parent TransTexas Healthcare. The banks of computers located at headquarters provided Scott, Ruth, Ron George, and the Executive Staff with on-line operational data which they presented to the group. This sharing was done by carefully contrasting the various rival field teams one to another so that fierce competition was assured between these already adversarial personality types. The ultimate failure for any of them, of course, was to be bested by an outsider. It was not considered permissible for any independent health care organization to defy the TransTexas Healthcare juggernaut.

One such acquisition target which was particularly resistant was Coastal Hospital. Scott himself decided to get involved after two of his emissaries had been summarily rebuffed. He arranged a one-on-one meeting with Frank Pierce, the CEO of this upstart not-for-profit, 300-bed community based hospital. He was surprised upon being ushered into his office to see an imposing, muscular, well-dressed, 40-year-old with a Boston accent, sitting behind a large, clean, wooden desk. Pierce didn't rise but motioned Scott towards a plain, small, straight chair located several yards in front of and off to the side of the desk. Scott debated remaining on his feet but did finally seat himself. "Mr. Richards, I know why you're here. I've reviewed your contract proposal, I've talked to friends at the Texas Hospital Association and convened a special board meeting so I don't think we should be anything less than straight in order that we don't waste each other's time." His rapid delivery and clipped eastern accent didn't even give Scott a chance to respond. "We don't believe you, we don't trust you or your organization, and we don't intend to have anything to do with you. We know we are at a competitive disadvantage, but by God, we won't go down easy. Now if you'll excuse me, I have work to do. My secretary will show you out." Pierce then turned his chair around and busily booted up his personal computer, leaving Scott with a view of the top of his head and the worn looking leather back of his chair. Simultaneously, the door opened and a secretary and a uniformed security guard who had obviously been listening on the intercom, entered the room.

"Mr. Richards, please follow me," the secretary announced in a broad Texas accent which sounded almost like an order, at the same time that the officer moved in behind Scott.

All right, very cute, thought Scott to himself. This might prove to be a chance to really play hardball and since he didn't ever intend to lose, this would be an opportunity to enhance the reputation of TransTexas Healthcare as having unbeatable strength. Furthermore, he loved the challenge of someone who for a change looked to be a worthy adversary. Most of the other hospital directors had been spineless wimps who had surrendered after the first fusillade. As he slid into the backseat of his Lear jet, he brought up a map of Texas covering the hundred miles within Coastal Hospital. His nearest TransTexas Healthcare Hospital was only 72 miles distant, not far by Texas standards, and he had two satellite "Doc-in-the-box" operations even closer. He picked up his sky phone and dialed the COO's office.

"Ron, Coastal stiffed me. We're going to need to teach them a little something about playing with the big boys and the best part of it is, we'll have an audience. They called the Texas Hospital Association in on us. Pull out the file and get Ruth and George to meet me at four o'clock in my office."

Scott replayed the Coastal conversation for his associates without going into how he had been out-maneuvered and dismissed, and then outlined his plan.

"Ron, we need to put a ring of satellite outpatient facilities around Coastal; they should open within six weeks. Move in our best docs, nurses and managers from wherever. These are going to be loss leaders—let's give free school vaccinations and hearing and vision tests for kids, and for adults free cholesterol tests, blood pressure screening and $10 mammograms and prostate exams, whatever we need to do to get the people in. Cost is not an issue; we'll write it off against the tax-free foundation as community service. Ruth, make sure that we get the funding straight. Now George, you're going to do some special 'public relations' work for Coastal." The ex-FBI agent looked puzzled. "Don't worry, all you have to do is start digging. I want dirt and I don't care how old it is. All the malpractice cases, no matter how they turned out; accidents; any violations in any inspection going back to day one, all such stuff. Then we need to go public, buy a reporter and somebody on the local television evening news. I want an expose on Coastal in the media. Get our Medical Affairs Office to recruit a group of current Coastal docs who will join us in three months. Big splash, offer them whatever." He was obviously enjoying himself as the strategy evolved. "I figure a few well-placed calls in four months to the state house ought to just about finish them, then we'll approach the hospital board of trustees directly and see if they think our money sounds better."

It actually took seven months but ended just as Scott had predicted. Coastal Hospital occupancy plummeted and as red ink accumulated into the millions the trustees reluctantly realized that they could accept TransTexas Healthcare as a "partner" or face bankruptcy in another 12-18 months. Calls from the Dallas Business Consortium to select board members, especially several to the chairman of the board, had helped, as had the nightly news investigation series now called "Coastal Watch" which had been a huge success. Gossipy tid-bits had been provided by several hospital employees who definitely liked supplementing their Coastal paychecks with TransTexas Healthcare money and whose lack of scruples had made them easily corruptible informants.

As Scott signed the acquisition contract, he noted that the soon to be former Coastal CEO was not present. Scott did receive, by messenger, an envelope the next day and it contained a terse handwritten note on Frank Pierce's personal stationery. It simply said, "You won the Coastal battle and you'll win others, but I believe that you'll lose the war. You and your pack are evil, and bad methods eventually give bad outcomes." Scott smiled. Talk is cheap, he thought to himself, as he surveyed his most recent triumph, although he wasn't quite done with this job, either.

He addressed the Coastal board at their next meeting and touted the new for-profit status, having made sure that his recently purchased television and newspaper reporters were present. He began as the video cameras started rolling, confidently standing next to an easel on which were a number of exhibits. "I am truly thrilled to be here and since our new partnership with Coastal came with some controversy, I wanted to meet you today to demonstrate that I am not a 20th century Lucifer, but just an American businessman like many of you. To begin with, let me just review what I believe is happening in health care today and why I am so excited to be involved. There is a revolution underway. The health care industry is becoming a competitive sector of the economy for the first time. Total costs are coming under control, quality is rising, some companies, hospitals, and individual practitioners are going under as they exit the industry. But as the saying goes, if you can't stand the heat, get out of the kitchen. Consolidated, integrated delivery systems are becoming the order of the day. Small-time medical care is collapsing. Health insurance, as we've known it, is dying. In TransTexas, we're looking at efficiency and effectiveness and flexibility and change and freedom. Furthermore," he now put on his most sincere demeanor, "we will be part of your community. We will be a big employer, as we have been everywhere we've gone in. And please remember that as a for-profit entity, we pay taxes, something that the old Coastal didn't do. Yes, we believe that profits in the health care marketplace are important in determining direction, since to be a successful organization we must have capital and consumer satisfaction, and satisfied customers make

THE LAST GRASP   **83**

it happen by paying us. As many of you know from your business, the market dynamic rules and I, for one, look forward to making our joint venture a success. I hope that you will join me. Thank you."

It played well to the audience, of which a majority were community businessmen. TransTexas Healthcare public relations made sure that the clips were seen on television stations throughout the five state area, usually as part of the health care news segment, not as a business story. This was the kind of publicity that would've been impossible to buy without the inside track that Scott already had purchased. Positive profiles of TransTexas Health Care started appearing in national as well as regional business publications, carefully couched in jargon that emphasized the positives of efficiency and market sensitivity and consumer satisfaction. Details of the funding and the bottom line were, of course, omitted since it was still a very private corporation.

TransTexas Healthcare did run into one barrier that they couldn't seem to overcome: a dispute that began when Scott found a distressed Catholic hospital in Fort Worth which had traditionally served the poor but was located in an area that had become gentrified and was surrounded by a ring of new high-rise apartment complexes and rehabbed single-family houses. An ideal market. After his team had made their initial contact, he received a phone call from the local Bishop's Secretariat saying that the Monsignor wanted to meet him at the soonest possible time. His initial response, on finding that his caller wanted to make the meeting on an urgent basis, was a mix of curiosity and satisfaction. Perhaps this could be a whole new opening for expansion and he decided that he would make this encounter a high priority. Two days later he shook hands with Monsignor Riley, who looked exactly like a classic, prototypical, scrappy, wiry, Irish parish priest should. This was not far off the mark. The prelate had grown up on Chicago's South Side and had been sent to Texas to address problems in discipline and finance that his predecessor had neglected.

The red-haired bantam prelate had barely settled into the throne-like chair, that Scott had arranged for him to use, when he began,

"Mr. Richards, I am here to tell you that I will not permit any further contacts between the diocese and TransTexas Healthcare and I mean to tell you why." Scott realized that the cannon certainly was not a man to mince words.

"Well, I appreciate your candor," Scott replied, still wondering if this might not be a negotiating ploy in what still had possibilities for gain. He found it hard to believe that everyone did not have a price.

Riley continued. "I am concerned in particular, with the commercialization of health care that you represent. The concept that there is no real difference between medical care and any other commodity like food, clothing, or shelter is, I believe, dead wrong. Nurses and doctors must be motivated by patient need, not the bottom line, if we are to have the benefits of a healthy community. Sick, vulnerable patients can't negotiate a price." Scott was surprised at this sophisticated business approach and only now recalled that his background check on Riley revealed that his guest had gotten an MBA from the School of Business at The University of Chicago.

The Bishop went on, "The purpose of medical care is cure, and if that's not possible, at least a cared-for patient who is comforted. Ultimately we aim for a healthier community. These concepts are the basic tenets of health care, not profits or return on investment for stock holders. When doctors and hospitals are at financial risk for providing treatment, there is no one left to advocate for the patient, especially when there's intense competition and under-treatment has great financial attractiveness. In addition, there are services that the communities always need but are unprofitable. For example, intensive care for premature babies of teenage mothers, or school immunization projects. Now I know that, because the neighborhood around St. Mary's has grown rich and is full of yuppies and married young people without children, it looks financially attractive for you, but let me ask you: In twenty years, if the neighborhood goes back to being a barrio with poor patients, will you stick around? Not likely!" He was leaning forward now with obvious passion in his voice. "That, sir, is why St. Mary's is prohibited from further discussions with your organization."

Scott had to admit he was impressed with the delivery, even though the message was not what he had expected or liked. No point in pushing it now, however. "Well, you said we should be frank, and frankly I do not agree. We don't ask the supermarkets to be responsible for feeding the poor and I don't feel responsible for their medical care. We may have further discussions and I'm sure we will still not agree but at least you've cleared the air and you should feel free to make an application to our charitable foundation for funding." Scott always liked to have the last word.

"We just might or we might not. We'll just have to wait and see," responded Monsignor Riley for his last word.

For the present, Scott was really much too busy to worry about taking on the Catholic Church; his Protestant religious upbringing provided the rationale for a pragmatic attitude and as Father Riley had said, just wait and see. TransTexas Healthcare now had 43 hospital based programs including three in Oklahoma, two in Louisiana and one in Arkansas. All in the course of only a little more than two years. The financial results, which were, as far as he was concerned, the best way to keep score, were spectacular. The Dallas Business Consortium was already receiving an incredible 104% annual return on investment. Ruth, brother-in-law Bill, and the employees who ran the numbers were hard pressed to hide this fact from the Internal Revenue Service. With such a four-star balance sheet, Scott had now become a peer to the Dallas Business Consortium Club, and he could hardly wait for their quarterly gathering, since, as always, he had a well defined business plan to present as their next leap.

CHAPTER 12

It was a typical June day in the District of Columbia, already hot and muggy at 8:30 a.m. when Dean Richard White entered the Rayburn Building, where the House Committee on Medical Affairs was holding their budget hearing on the new health funding proposals. To even the most knowledgeable beltway insiders, these sounded like the dullest of proceedings. Given the stakes, however, nothing could have been further from the truth. The provisions of House bills dealing with the National Institute of Health and state funding for Medicaid were indeed mundane and unchanged from previous years. What was very different were requests for statutes permitting deregulation of the for-profit companies which had started forming integrated medical systems such as TransTexas Healthcare. In the best tradition of capitalism, at issue was a proposal to remove rules requiring government oversight which would encourage an unbridled, corporate, medical entrepreneurial atmosphere. Scott Richards and the Dallas Business Consortium had been most helpful to the sponsors of the bill, both in suggesting its content and in supporting their campaign financing. Doctor White, as a representative of the Association of

Medical School Deans, was in town to testify against the very provisions of the bill that Richards and his partners had introduced in the legislation.

He began with the usual credentialing statement about himself and the organization he represented and then went into his testimony. "I am here on behalf, not only of this country's medical schools, but also to speak for the patients, especially those politically silent and disadvantaged groups that I saw when I was practicing at the Metro County Hospital. This bill will make it certain that, in only a few years, a few mega corporations will skim the employed healthy population into their plans, leaving those unable to fend for themselves on the outside of the system looking in. If we have another recession and unemployment increases, the number of those who lack health insurance will skyrocket, Medicaid will be overburdened in every state, and the human toll measured in worsened U.S. health will be staggering. This bill doesn't level the field, it tilts it heavily in favor of healthcare systems already getting too big and having too much say."

"Now, Dean White," interjected Congressman Dwight (D Texas), "I fail to see a problem with what looks to be simply a classic, American, business solution to a rapidly emerging financial problem."

White's external composure was unchanged, though his emotional temperature was rising rapidly. "With all due respect, Congressman," he said, "providing medical care is not a business. It's a calling to service. Equating it to the making of widgets is, in my opinion, a dangerous approach that assures a self-fulfilling prophesy. Profit incentives will lead to destruction of an equal opportunity in terms of access to health care. Healthcare is a mirror of society's concern for justice, compassion and its soul. I believe that this bill tears apart the very heart of our society."

"Thank you, Dean White," interjected the chair of the committee. "We appreciate your taking the time to speak with us." And with that curt dismissal, he gaveled the meeting into adjournment.

Later that night, Scott's private line rang. "Mr. Richards?" asked a young enthusiastic voice.

"Yes, and who the hell are you?"

"I'm calling for Representative Dwight who wishes to speak with you."

"Get him on the phone now, young lady." A pause ensued.

"Hello, Scott."

"Ralph, Goddamnit, if you are going to use this line, do it yourself. Don't have *Tinkerbell* call. Now what is it?"

"The bill will go through okay, but there was a guy here today testifying in opposition who was scary. He's a medical school dean by the name of White. He's really dangerous sounding. Stuff about making access available for everyone and alleging that groups like yours are skimming. Claims to represent a bunch of medical school deans. I had him looked up. He's apparently got good credentials, but he sounds like a goddamn socialist to me."

"Don't be so antsy. I know the Academic University type. Lots of talk, usually no action. But I'll follow it up."

And he did. What Scott got was a report on a man who really did live up to his principles and his writing and public statements showed that he was consistently committed to a broad based approach to the delivery of medical care. It was clear that he did not put up with fools. White's standards were very high, and his tolerance for what he perceived as incompetence or injustice was zero. Scott was amused when the evaluation arrived. "Hard to believe that such old fashioned thinking still gets men into important positions these days," he said dismissively.

A few days later, Scott was very pleased when he received an invitation to attend the Woods Conference. He had first heard of this annual event during his early days at McCloud, McGlory and Johnson. He recalled how happy one of the senior partners had been to have been invited into this prestigious fraternity, and how impressed the other partners had been. Upon inquiry about why this was such a big deal, he had learned that this was more or less a self-selected all male group who considered themselves to be the movers and shakers of commerce and industry in the nation. They gathered for three days at a retreat north of San Francisco to hear presentations from futurists and to make contacts which allowed for significant networking and horse trading in a neutral environment, devoid of the usual pressures and legal oversights. The sociability engendered in such a gathering replete with gourmet meals and the best in wines and other libations was reputed to be a setting that spawned many gentlemen's agreements which later blossomed into formal, mutually beneficial, major commercial contracts. For Scott, this was a distinction that came at the right time. He had been carefully observing how Sam Walton and all of the other low-cost retailers had changed the entire field of merchandising. In the same way, he knew that what he was about was changing the face of medical care and he expected that the Woods group would offer him new insights and opportunities for beneficial connections.

He was not disappointed. Shortly after his arrival, he found himself involved in discussions with CEOs of major medical supply houses, insurance companies and drug manufacturers. Fertile opportunities for collaboration abounded and Scott, although a new inductee, was not reluctant to work the room to his benefit. The other attendees were, of course, likewise engaged and such encounters made for extremely animated exchanges which sometimes became active debates rather than thoughtful deliberations, but in the final analysis, all parties usually left feeling very well served.

CHAPTER 13

Scott was addressing the quarterly meeting of the Dallas Business Consortium, having announced that he had the investment opportunity of the decade to lay out before them.

"Gentlemen and partners." The group appreciated the fact that Scott had, at every opportunity, availed himself of stock options instead of cash bonuses. "I believe we here at TransTexas are well positioned to take the next logical step, leveraging our current position to such an extent that our present situation, as attractive as it seems, will be looked upon as minimal. We should go national and go public."

"National," okay, the group was used to that, but they considered "public" to be dangerous in their scheme of things. That's something they'd have to think about. In their world, this was risky not so much because of concern about government interventions but because it had more to do with their peers, the other business groups in health care who would not welcome any new intrusions which had the potential to destabilize the existing system. It was, in effect, like beginning a new, huge automobile company in the face of Ford,

Chrysler, and GM. Scott sensed their discomfort. However, this was an essential step if they expected to dominate the U.S. health care industry, and he knew this was a defining moment. He continued, with renewed determination.

"The health care insurance market has grown fat," he said. "It's really just an old boys' club, where no one has had to do anything inventive for decades except defend the status quo. We have the opportunity to launch a pre-emptive strike which will make 15% of the national budget available to us; that's four or five percent of all of the money spent in the whole world! It's all within your grasp, if we do what I'm proposing. I am here to tell you that this makes the Morgans, the Mellons, the Vanderbilts, and the Rockefellers look like pikers. Think about it for a moment. Look at the returns from TransTexas. Using that, we can leverage a stock plan where you'll have minimal risk and tremendous potential. If we simply replicate TransTexas Healthcare into the South, Mid-Atlantic and Midwest, that's over 120 million customers and believe me, the employers will love us. We can use our track record to prove that we can reduce costs while improving their profitability and competitiveness."

The group had to admit that Scott had helped their own parent organization do just that, and their colleagues in business were more than pleased with TransTexas Healthcare. True, their reduced services for some of the sick had resulted in occasional complaints, but what the hell, you have to crack a few eggs to make an omelet. As a group, they certainly liked being compared to the Rockefellers and Vanderbilts; it was quite appealing.

"A major opportunity like this hasn't been available in this country for over a hundred years," Scott continued. "It will certainly not come again in our lifetime. Think of it, $750 billion at stake, three-quarters of a trillion waiting to be captured and with almost no downside risk. Remember, you will be the major stock holders. Even though we're public, you'll be able to call the tune." Scott knew he had to push the right buttons for this group, and he did. Their collective acquisitive appetites and the dangled bait was more than they could resist.

"Well, if we did this, how would you sequence it?" drawled Sam Johnson. That question was all Scott needed. Using the carefully crafted overheads, which had been re-revised and revised by his legal and accounting staffs literally hundreds of times until perfect, Scott launched into a 90-minute discussion on a three year strategic battle plan which outlined specifics of the timeline, milestones, goals and objectives, and tactics. The legal aspects were complex due to the public stock status, but the Dallas Business Consortium would indeed be able to control the conglomerate. Basically it was just County Health Plan taken to a national scale, and Scott had certainly shown that he knew how to do that successfully. The group was now fully engaged, sitting upright with each individual entrepreneur calculating how this would enhance his own financial situation. The room was electric with energy that was almost palpable.

"This is a nice opening, Scott," Charlie said. "Of course, we must present this to our lawyers and CFOs but I most assuredly agree that it's got to be kept strictly confidential, only within this group. I move we reconvene in one week to come to a decision after whatever due diligence we each have to undertake." The motion carried unanimously.

Scott was elated. He knew his plan was flawless and would pass even the most minute scrutiny. After all, his lawyers and accountants came from the same top-tier schools as their advisors and the teams he had trained were now tested veterans of hospital takeovers so he knew it could be done once he had the capital. In just a week, he hoped that his ambitious dream would become a reality.

When the group reconvened each of them had used their organization's resources to extensively review Scott's detailed business plan. Their financial and legal advisors had discussed methods of financing via their financial banking alliances in Little Rock, the Bahamas and New York City. Scott's prediction was quite correct: since all these consultants had gone to the same schools and had the same background and experiences and had all grown up in the age of takeovers, mergers and acquisitions, they liked it. It was a good deal, carefully crafted by Scott's staff and well-timed. The result, therefore,

THE LAST GRASP 93

was never in question. A unanimous agreement to move rapidly was the conclusion. TransNational Healthcare was a reality! Scott was, of course, ecstatic. Exactly where he wanted to be at the right time, with the capital to carry it off.

Other men might have celebrated or taken a breather before starting such a major undertaking, but not Scott. He used the next Sunday management meeting, which the attendees now referred to as prayer sessions, to put the plan into operation. The management group was more than ready, they were truly energized since they were Scott clones, both by nature and by the fact that they had been trained by an expert. No group of warriors had ever gotten better combat preparation. They had been carefully recruited and trained. To each of them, the thrill of pursuit, the cutting of the deal, and the jubilation of victory were powerful, almost aphrodisiac incentives. In addition, there was the money, which was, by any standards, generous. Only the most senior accountants, however, really understood just how much money was flowing into the organization as a result of the efforts of these high-achieving work teams. Now Scott stood in front of them in an uncharacteristically jovial mood, in his shirt sleeves. Although he allowed them to come to the meeting in informal dress, he always had his tailored suit and designer tie uniform on, and most followed his example.

He began his invocation, "This is a crucial moment for all of us, the future is ours to grasp." He went on to outline the specifics of what needed to be done with the timeline and milestones to sequence the tasks for each division. A vastly increased workforce was clearly something necessary, meaning each of them would have significantly increased duties and responsibilities. As the clincher, Scott reviewed the enormous financial potential of the TransNational Healthcare stock option plan, knowing that this opportunity would energize them like no other workforce in the country. He was right; they were dazzled.

"Questions?" he asked, having completed his tour de force presentation.

"How will we be using mergers and acquisitions to help us grow?" asked an intense young man sitting on the edge of his chair in the first row.

"Simple question," Scott began. "We will of course use that tactic, but will choose the ones that fall into our lap. There are both big name and no name health-care providers that are ripe for takeover. We have a line on all of them . . . and when the time is right, we'll pick them up for a song." The young man was suitably chagrined by such a put-down. Obviously the boss considered that this was a kindergarten level inquiry.

"How about the threat of health care reform?" someone asked. "Some congressmen and physician groups like the American College of Physicians and the Physicians for a National Health Program are calling for total system restructuring; even proposing a government single payer, like the Canadian system. This would be a problem, wouldn't it?" This question came from a woman dressed in an expensive Gucci outfit.

"Very good question, Jean." Scott knew her name since they had entertained one another one night in Amarillo following a successful local hospital conquest. "This is something we'll have to watch closely. The Physicians for a National Health Program are academics and fuzzy-headed socialists. They're only potentially dangerous. The American College of Physicians is big and their plan is well-crafted, but it's vulnerable, since they are too altruistic and focus primarily on trying to help patients. Congress is not a problem unless we get a president who pushes them. Bill Clinton is considering a run for president and is making noises about health care, but he'll never get nominated much less elected. This area will require watching and if it heats up, we'll have to put in some money to help shape the process."

There were no more questions. Each person reviewed their personal copy of their assignments which grew out of the strategic plan. As they went out into the Sunday afternoon Texas fall sunshine most retired to their offices, not to their homes. They continued to be energized by the day's events as they individually began their work on

THE LAST GRASP

the projects which would secure the future success of TransNational Healthcare.

Three days later, Scott was somewhat surprised to see that his Vice President for medical affairs had requested a special private meeting. Scott considered him crucial to operations since he had demonstrated credibility in the medical world and had been effective in assuring the efficient functioning of the medical aspects of TransTexas Healthcare. Scott really felt that as technicians, doctors all demanded too much money. However, he believed that the marketplace would ultimately solve this problem too, as recent surveys were starting to suggest. And besides, this physician had never really made the type of aggressive demands that Scott was used to receiving from other senior employees.

"What can I do for you, John?" Scott began the discussion amicably. The balding, slightly paunchy physician who looked the part of a kindly family doctor handed Scott an envelope.

"What's this?"

"Read it and see. It's my letter of resignation. I'm done."

For once Scott was surprised. He considered this might be a ploy for squeezing out more salary dollars.

"I joined you and TransTexas Healthcare because I believed that it was the wave of the future," he said. "I thought it would be something good that could keep the system from strangling. I hoped it would eventually provide affordable care for more people while controlling costs. You and my fellow Vice Presidents seem to have abandoned the human side of how your decisions impact people—or as you refer to them, customers or covered lives. Initially we went after a fat system, now however, you're down to cutting muscle and bone. When you set up strategies that save money, we're basically just slashing care for people any which way we can. When we send new mothers home 18 hours after delivery, we're jeopardizing the health of two people. When we require that patients call to get approval for emergency department visits we have to know that many times it just won't happen, and that care is being denied. I didn't go to medical school to spend my career denying care to patients. I can't be part of a system that refers to providing care for sick patients as medically related losses. I've got a new position with a medium-sized group practice. where I'll be seeing individual patients one at a time until you or somebody else puts us out of business. but at least I'll sleep well at night."

"Bully for you." Scott said. "But you don't have two weeks. you're done now. And I don't accept your letter. you're fired. You've got thirty minutes to clean out your desk and be off the premises or security will do it for you. So don't let the door hit you in the ass." Scott's face was white with anger now. "If I ever hear that you've voiced any public criticism of TransTexas Healthcare or me or anyone else in the organization. I'll see to it that you're destroyed. And don't think I can't do it!" he roared at the physician who had turned on his heel and withdrawn. leaving Scott to contemplate his replacement. a man he'd already been researching.

Jack Johnson. M.D. was a true company man. never having seen a real patient since his internship. With an MBA and five years of HMO management experience he was the perfect new Vice-President for Medical Affairs at TransNational. No chance of his defecting into the practice of medicine: after all. he didn't ever really know how to do it in the first place and he had long since bought into the industrial model as the gospel for health care and health care delivery.

That evening the ex-medical director described his personal sense of liberation to his wife as the Armstrongs shared a quiet dinner and contemplated their new circumstances. "After all." he said. "how many men are fortunate enough to be able to undo a devil's pact during their time on earth?"

CHAPTER 14

WTTW, the public television station in Chicago was sponsoring a live round-table titled "The Future of Medical Care in the Decade Ahead." Participants included a heart transplant surgeon from California, a virologist from New York City, Scott Richards and Dean Richard White. The moderator was a Vice President for Public Affairs from the AMA. White was surprised to see Scott in person. As usual, Richards was impeccably dressed in a custom tailored suit that undoubtedly cost more than the Dean's entire closet wardrobe, but he was physically less impressive than the dominant personality the Dean had expected. The evening began in a benign manner with the heart surgeon and the virologist predicting great science-based medical breakthroughs. Scott joined in predicting a wonderful new, efficient era for organized medicine with TransNational Healthcare as an example of the ideal new delivery system for the age. The AMA representative beamed. It was then White's turn.

"I hate to be the skunk at the garden party," he began. "But I believe that we've already entered into a spiral of disaster that negates all the quite remarkable current scientific advances which my two colleagues have described and of which they're justifiably so very proud. Most of these are directly attributable to the work at academic medical centers. But if Mr. Richards and the other large organizations gain financial control of the key elements of the system, they will kill research and development and emasculate medical care as we know it! They're well on the way to doing that, already; if they decide to get a string of funeral homes, they'd about have it all!"

The AMA representative looked convulsed. "I don't think you're being quite fair, Dr. White," he interjected.

"On the contrary, I have the incontrovertible weight of fact and evidence on my side."

"Oh really?" Scott began. "You make profit sound like a four-letter word. Is that part of your political belief? Capitalism is after all what built this country and has kept communism at bay. Do you like the Russian and Chinese and Cuban systems and want to see them here? Do you, Doctor?" Scott had lost his usual smooth veneer.

"Of course not," White snapped. "That's the most ridiculous contrast you can draw, isn't it? What scares me is that profit is becoming the dominant consideration in most medical decisions. It will prostitute all legitimate medical concerns for patients."

"Did you call me and my organization prostitutes?" Scott had completely lost all semblance of control and was on his feet.

"No, but if the shoe fits. . . ."

The moderator was also on his feet now, between the two combatants, while the other two panelists sat open mouthed. "Gentlemen, gentlemen, let me remind you where we are and what we came here to discuss."

The producer sitting only a few feet away behind a glass partition had cut off the microphones to both adversaries and was hissing into the earpiece receiver of the moderator that neither of them was to talk during the remaining seven minutes of the program. The show ended uneventfully.

"Well, Doctor, we will most certainly meet again and the outcome will not likely be a neutral one," was Scott's parting shot.

BS

"No doubt," was the Dean's taciturn response. He was contemplating what some of the University trustees might be thinking if they had viewed the program or would see a tape of it. Controversy was generally not well received at Southeastern. Of an even more pressing concern, he also worried about the reception he would get when he arrived home. His wife was sometimes critical of his tendency, as she described it, "never to leave a medical windmill untilted at." When he came off the jetway at the regional airport, she was there with, of all things, a huge smile and a kiss to match.

"Honey, I have never been more proud of you," was her only comment. Following which she launched into a discussion of the most recent adventures and achievements of their children at their schools.

The next morning, Dean White was back at work looking forward to doing one of the things he loved best: teaching. As dean, there were many other demands on his time, but since he was always talking to the faculty about leadership by example, he knew that it was crucial for him to show that not only did he lecture about what doctors should do, but also that he could actually do it. Besides, with the uncertainties of having a dean's job these days, he appreciated that it was always prudent to keep your doctoring skills updated. Therefore at 7:30 a.m. he was meeting with the team of students and residents on Ward 4 South of the University hospital. The group felt they were well prepared for the session of rounds. The students had practiced, more than once, their presentations on the new patients' medical histories and physical examination findings and the residents had reviewed the most recent medical journal articles on the unusual aspects of some of the more interesting patients under their care. In spite of this, they were a bit nervous, since it was well known that the dean was always full of surprises as he went about making his teaching points. As it turned out, this morning was to continue his tradition of doing the unexpected.

Instead of asking them about their most interesting, challenging or esoteric problems, the dean picked out the thickest chart from the pile on the table in the conference room. He thumbed through it briefly and said. "Please tell me about Mr. Farquar. It looks as if he's been here a long time."

The young physicians were taken aback since this was not one of the patients they'd boned up on. There was an uncomfortable silence.

"Well, actually, he's sort of a street person who's eight days post myocardial infarction and is just waiting to go home," said Dr. Monica Jackson, the senior resident, as she looked around the room for help from her other team members.

"He's really stable, nothing very exciting," added Tom Rielly, the intense junior resident.

"Let's go visit him anyhow," was the dean's response as they moved to Mr. Farquar's bedside.

"Mr. Farquar, they tell me you're going home soon, and I was just wondering where home was and who'd be looking after you when you move out of the hospital, helping you with your meals and your medicine," White said.

Mr. Farquar was a tall bearded mountaineer type and was obviously enjoying the attention. "Doc, before I got into here I was sleeping in the back seat of an '88 Caddy on a used car lot where one of my old buddies works. Just me and the watchdogs at night. I guess I'll go back there; I've got a hot plate and an electric fry pan for the cooking, unless you got a better plan."

"Maybe we do," said the dean as he turned to address the uniformly embarrassed group of young physicians. "You've done a technically great job with Mr. Farquar. He's on aspirin and a Beta blocker for prevention and an ACE inhibitor for his heart failure. But you really blew it with his social history and plans for post hospital care follow-up. What do you think your next move should be?"

Dr. Jackson had now regained her composure and said, "I guess we'd better get an emergency social work consult and talk about arranging a short term place for him to live and get some diet and lifestyle education started and make sure home health is involved from day one and that we get him an early follow-up clinic appointment."

"What do you think of all that, Mr. Farquar?" White asked.

"Well, sounds okay, but I've tried it all before. I think I'd like to do it my way as Frank Sinatra says in his song," was the reply.

"You're certainly not crazy or incompetent, so we can't force you into anything that you don't think is right for you," said White. "Just one more question, though, please tell us about your family."

"Don't know about 'em anymore. They kinda get disgusted with me about my drinkin' a few years back. I've give up booze now, but too late I guess. Dunno' what happened to my son who left a year after my wife died from breast cancer. She was 47, it spread like wildfire, they couldn't do anything 'cept make her comfortable." Mr. Farquar was obviously having trouble with his composure and paused as his voice stuttered with emotion.

"People to whom things like that happen often try to ward off their depression with alcohol, Mr. Farquar," the dean said. "It's not moral weakness, it's depression which is a very real medical disease. How's your appetite and sleep and how good is your concentration now and how often do you feel really blue?"

"Doc, you really got me figured. All those things are bad. I wish I could do it again different," the patient replied.

"Dean White, could I please ask him a question?" said Deborah Murray, a black medical student who had been standing quietly in her white coat, in the back row of those surrounding the bedside. She was a short, serious looking, young woman with glasses, whose tremulous voice hinted that she was somewhat intimidated by having to speak up to the dean.

"Certainly," said White, "Mr. Farquar and I are all ears."

"Mr. Farquar," said the student, "is your son named Donald?"

"Why, yes, how did you know?"

"Well, I just got off the obstetrical service here three days ago and a Mr. and Mrs. Donald Farquar just had triplets, and in the joyous moments in the delivery room, when babies and mother were all doing well, I heard him make a touching comment to one of the nurses about how much he wished his parents could have been part of the event. I guess he thinks you must have died too, since he hadn't heard from you."

Mr. Farquar was now completely overcome with tears and was unable to respond. Dean White took charge.

"Thank you so much, Ms. Murray, good work! Good news don't you think, Mr. Farquar? It seems like you've got some very good reasons now to take care of your heart, doesn't it? Ms. Murray, do you think the Farquar triplets are still here?"

"Oh yes, they won't be discharged for at least a few more days."

"Good. I'm sure that we can arrange a visit for a proud grandfather, and we'll see to it that Donald Farquar finds out about this and we'll arrange a reunion, right?" Dean White said.

"You bet. I'll do it this morning," said the student, now glowing with pride.

"Sounds too good to be true. Thanks to all of you I've really gotten a second chance on life, thank you. Thank you," was Mr. Farquar's final comment as the team moved onto the next patient.

"A great lesson for all of us as to why it's such a privilege to do what we do," was the dean's summary comment on this particular episode which became a human interest feature that night on the local television news broadcast.

CHAPTER 15

TransNational Healthcare burst upon the scene, shaking the health care world so that even the big boys were impressed. It was working just as Scott had hoped. It had all been carefully coordinated as a result of his meticulous plan and everyone had carried out their assignments flawlessly. The general counsel's office had done well; in particular, assistant counsel Ken Franklin had been notably effective in getting the prospectus approved by the Securities Exchange Commission oversight group. He was an intense, sandy-haired, serious, young man with wire rimmed glasses who seldom smiled, but was indeed possessed of great intellectual talents and a unique ability to write and speak business talk, something seldom seen in corporate attorneys. Scott commented upon this to his Chief Counsel at the next senior management meeting. "I couldn't agree more about his skills, though I wish he wouldn't worry so much about what's going to happen to the people involved in some of the consolidations," Thomas said. Scott made a note to ensure that the young attorney was used to advantage in future undertakings, especially if the Feds were to be significantly involved in reviewing the outcomes of the negotiations.

TransNational Healthcare had moved their executive and financial offices to New York City which meant that Anne no longer had to commute to Dallas for obligatory social events. In her familiar surroundings and environment she could call the tune, at least in setting the format of their and social entertaining engagements, and could extract from her husband the appearance of a conventional marriage, and from his colleagues the respect due the wife of a rising star in the charged atmosphere of Wall Street. The competitive, publicity-seeking, conspicuous consumption of the high flying entrepreneurs who inhabited the pages of *W* and *Town and Country* suited her very well and the almost unlimited budget that she enjoyed was a decided perk of her current station. She was by now well aware that her husband had not been faithful to his wedding vows, but given the alternatives of overlooking such transgressions and maintaining her present life with its benefits and opulence or a divorce settlement in obscurity, she felt there was no contest. Besides, over the past several years, her focus had never really left New York. With initial contacts from her family, her legendary parties and gregarious instincts, her participation in New York society and the associations that had flowed through her husband's business interactions, it was apparent that she had a large number of friends of both sexes. Several men, in particular, over the months had been happy to share time with her in the Richards' luxurious penthouse bedroom and the personal reinforcement of their attentions plus the fact that their lovemaking seemed somehow more thoughtful, considerate and intimate than that of her husband, gave her considerable pleasure as well as physical gratification.

While Anne was working hard at her society and social activities, her husband and TransNational Healthcare were capturing an ever increasing segment of Wall Street health care activities. Favorable profiles appeared in all the major financial periodicals and the stock which had initially been publicly offered at $15 a share was, after only four months, up to almost $50 on the New York Stock Exchange. The strategy of translating the tactics perfected at County Health Network and TransTexas Healthcare had easily shifted to the

THE LAST GRASP

national model. The hiring and personnel practices for takeovers were reproduced. All of his fellow healthcare executives had to start worrying about the TransNational effect on their businesses. This was exactly how Scott wanted it.

The Dallas Business Consortium was more than delighted, they were ecstatic. With good reason! They never had enjoyed such profits. Even in their most successful oil ventures, there had been dry wells and restrictions on the number of cubic feet that could be extracted per hour by each well, and unpredictable dramatic shifts in the market price were always a problem. None of this unpredictability existed in the health-care business. And while the petroleum business had average profits at roughly 20-25% per year, TransNational Healthcare was turning a 230% annual return on investment. It was better than a printing press and all completely legal. They were awash in money, and with such a run up on the stock they were able to raise huge capital reserves to deal with any hospitals or competing companies simply by selling more stock. Their enthusiasm was unbridled, as was their appreciation of Scott. However, they realized that anonymity was crucial and they insisted that there should be a dummy corporation to distance them from the fast emerging TransNational Healthcare behemoth. Grudgingly, Scott permitted the formation of U.S. Enterprises with Ron George, the COO of TransNational Healthcare listed as its director. It was, of course, just a money laundering shell to use as a pass-through conduit. Ruth as Chief Financial Officer kept track of the wire transfers, signing on substantial paperwork for the deposits in the Dallas Business Consortium designated banks in Little Rock and New York, as well as their captive treasuries offshore in the Caribbean.

As the profits of TransNational Healthcare escalated, Scott Richards indulged himself by founding the Little Rock Youth Alliance. Like its creator, its origins were complex. He still felt very keenly the early neglect and rejection by his father in a very personal way and this emotional and physical deprivation was something that needed to be undone. He felt somehow that the Alliance would be yet another demonstration of how erroneous his father's dismal predications about him had been. On a practical level, it also served multiple other purposes. It deflected potential local, negative perceptions of his business operations, showing what he was doing for his community, and it of course took maximum advantage of the tax laws to be certain that it didn't cost many real dollars. Finally, he truly liked the image of the local boy who had made good and was returning resources to the community. Strange how raw the scars were, so that he still needed to vindicate himself as a winner to alleviate his private distress.

The goal of the Alliance was "to enhance the possibilities for young Americans, especially those from the south, to enter the business world by expanding educational opportunities for them." Candidates were required to be "intelligent and astute and to come from meager financial circumstances in settings of difficult home situations." Clearly Scott considered himself to be the prototypical model person for such a program. He did openly appreciate the fact that he himself had been advantaged by his educational experiences at Columbia which had truly changed his life, and he sent them some money too. He also used his considerable organizational talents to develop the framework for his Little Rock charity, drawing upon the pieces of TransNational Healthcare for its management, legal and financial structure. The central office in Little Rock encouraged candidates from all 50 states to apply, so that every fall each public high school in the country received a glossy brochure inviting nominees to compete for designation as scholars of the Little Rock National Youth Alliance. Besides the criteria of being from poor, disadvantaged, difficult home situations, they should have personal characteristics of "dedication to work, a future promise of success and must demonstrate the ambition and potential to be a prominent American of the next century."

The thousands of applications, letters of recommendations and transcripts were sorted through with the most promising being forwarded for final review by a multidisciplinary group of educators, businessmen and scientists. Annually, over three hundred such individuals were eventually identified and given scholarships. Scott actually felt great satisfaction and pleasure from this endeavor, much beyond the public relations and tax advantages that it provided. He would on occasion reflect on what else he might do in a similar vein. However, the business at hand and the competitive juices always seemed to overtake such altruistic contemplations.

One problem that Scott had not anticipated was the fact that Bill Clinton had indeed been elected President and furthermore, it appeared that he was serious about health care reform which could be a real problem for the mega hospital conglomerates such as TransNational, as well as for the established HMOs, and the for-profit health insurance companies. Scott reviewed the situation with the senior management group as they sat in their newly completed oak paneled boardroom, which featured one thirty-foot picture window facing uptown Manhattan and Central Park, and a slightly larger one overlooking Wall Street.

He began, "The implications of the proposed health care changes could be monumental for us; our growth rate has already started to flatten because of the uncertain future. As we all know, some of our success is due to the fact that we are able to pick and choose our customers, signing up only those who are healthy enough to be employed. If we're forced to take a certain number of indigents and of all-comers, as the Clintons propose, we're screwed. We'll be lucky to turn a double digit profit."

A look at the grim faces around the table assured Scott that the problem was indeed understood by all present. A prolonged and quite thoughtful political/economic discussion followed. A tiered response was gradually crafted. What evolved was a true strategic masterpiece, not surprisingly, since this was clearly one of the best health care think tank groups in the business. One thing Scott knew was that the academic crowd Hillary Clinton had convened to address the problem was no match for his experts in terms of experience, focus, and knowledge. The major tactic was to play on the widespread distrust of the American government, by utilizing methods already put in place by the health insurance industry. They envisioned a series of follow-up advertisements with comparisons of the Clinton plan to the

Post Office or IRS, misinformation pieces with implied threats of disrupted physician choice, reduced quality of care, ominous comments about restrictions and reductions of Medicare benefits. It was to be alleged that it would bankrupt the country by giving preferential care to minorities and a flood of immigrants.

As the campaign unfolded, it appeared to be going well, but it was difficult to be sure since powerful forces were at work. Many of the large, multi-national businesses were intrigued by the Clinton plan, which would have substantially benefited their bottom line by reducing the direct costs of providing health insurance for their employees, but all were afraid to commit. Anxiety was rampant, especially for some of the younger, faint-at-heart health-care executives who seemed ready to run and panic, cutting deals and capitulating to what seemed to be the inevitability of a government funded program. Scott sensed an opportunity, and with a few well placed phone calls he had established himself as the convener of a health care funding summit which was to be held in a luxury southwestern mountain retreat. The public title of this meeting was "Creating a Public/Private Partnership to Enhance the Health Care of America." This, of course, was simply a cover for a clandestine meeting of CEOs of most of the major health care players to discuss the problems presented by the Clintons' health care reform, although to admit such a thing would of course have been totally illegal under anti-trust. He recruited several prominent academic health economists and ex-government health care administrators to give "keynote addresses" and convene open forum seminars which were to be well attended by minor functionaries in the various organizations. The real action was of course taking place in the private conference room where the seniors convened. Scott Richards gave the keynote address here!

"Don't get unstrung," was the reassuring message. "The Force is With Us" was the title of his speech. He was indeed a master at leading such an undertaking and was in his glory as he stood at the head of the table of well tailored, mostly silver-haired, executive attendees. He was well into the control mode that suited him perfectly.

"You're a bunch of wimps!" he chided them. "The Clinton plan was devised by a group of Ph.Ds led by Hillary. Though well-meaning, they're all naive and had little or no experience or understanding of how patient care is delivered. The President, while correct in thinking that health care financing is a concern to multiple constituencies, doesn't really understand that health care doesn't follow the usual laws of economics. Since demand is currently unrestricted and we can control the supply, as long as the demand exists we're in the driver's seat. The only thing we have to fear is demand reduction or control of prices, and nothing in the current health reform program proposes that. Americans all deny death and consider unrestricted access to health care as an entitlement. You're the biggest group of nervous nellies I've ever seen," he told them. "The worst case scenario is that we private healthcare providers will get some regulations."

"We should basically see this only as a speed bump," Ruth said. "Let's get down to the business at hand, which is to control the market and be certain that we don't get too many bad accounts." The room was silent. Clearly Scott had impressed the group and established himself as a dominant force in this small and very exclusive fraternity. As their next agenda items, they got down to discussing the effectiveness of their marketing and advertising strategies to counter reform, with plans to support political candidates who would be willing to let the marketplace be the metaphor for health care. After a final summary the gathering dispersed. Of course, no minutes were kept of this meeting which, if anyone inquired, had never happened.

The closing social event for the conference was a luxury cookout with a black-tie wait staff serving the attendees, some of whom looked very out of place and uncomfortable in their recently purchased western attire. It was an impressive setting, however, high on a mesa on a clear night with unlimited vistas and a ceiling of moon and the stars. Scott felt highly satisfied with the outcome of his undertaking and performance. He believed that, like the horizon, his future was unlimited.

Although TransNational Healthcare was looking more and more like it could do anything it wished, all was not well within its internal structure. In the first place the dramatic increase in size meant that Scott had less ability to be on top of all aspects of the operations. Even though his travel schedule remained frenetic, and the traditional Sunday meetings were expanded so that they often lasted into the evening, assuring that he had total control was still a problem. Ron George was frequently singled out for public criticism at meetings and he bridled under what he considered extremely unjust and uncalled for negative comments. One Sunday night, after a contentious senior management meeting, he and Scott confronted one another across Scott's altar-like desk. "I don't like being always publicly whipped in these sessions and I don't deserve it," Ron said. "It's all well and good for you to be flying around the country, but I'm here at headquarters making day-to-day decisions so that the business prospers. Are you trying to do to me in front of the others, what you do to Ruth in private?" He suddenly realized that he had gone too far even though Scott's continuing, though infrequent sexual liaisons with the chief financial officer, were not exactly a secret.

"Watch it," Scott said. "You're good but not indispensable. And you're damnwell paid, too. Don't forget it. I'm not about to change how I run things and whenever I think you've screwed up I'll tell you about it wherever we are." Both parties fell temporarily silent. Ron knew that he was well paid and he wasn't about to throw his seven figure salary away without an alternative. Scott also knew that Ron was right, that for the present at least, his COO was critical for the day-to-day operations and might truly almost be irreplaceable at this moment. Scott broke the silence, "Look, we've both had a hard day and a tough year. Let's go get a drink and forget it. Besides, the truth is that Ruth is basically a mercy fuck and always has been. I'll just forget your comment."

"Okay," George said. "We've had a hard day, let's just forget it." In reality, George was not about to forget any of this. In the first place he knew that the mercy fuck comment could at some time be very useful, since he had no reason to believe Scott wasn't serious. Second, he also appreciated how really vulnerable Scott was. Finally, it was not his nature to forget, much less to forgive.

At the same time, unbeknownst to Scott, another problem had arisen. It involved his brother-in-law and it began innocently enough. Ordinarily, travel and entertainment expenses went through the accounts payable department on a routine basis. However, as a result of staff reductions due to illness and vacations, responsibility for reimbursement had been temporarily shifted to general accounting and any charges over five thousand dollars required a sign-off by a senior manager.

One week this duty fell to Bill, who had received a large sheaf of vouchers from the preceding months, which he dutifully took to methodically initialing. For some reason he started to see a pattern where Scott was consistently paired one-on-one with mid-level female staff, sometimes for one trip, sometimes for several in a row. He found this both curious and troubling. Actually, he had always been ambivalent about Scott. Clearly he respected Scott on one level, but at the same time, he was repulsed by his aggressiveness and insensitivity. His brother-in-law believed that the desired ends justified virtually any means. It also clearly bothered Bill that not only had his sister married such a man, but he himself had also enthusiastically gone to work for him. He sometimes mused over what Scott thought of them and what commitment, if any, he felt towards them, especially towards Anne, for whom Bill still felt a protective responsibility, something that started following their parent's death. It was the latter emotion which generated a need for follow-up of his initial observations, even though he had handled only a single batch of vouchers and the regular channels were once again utilized when the accounts-payable staff got back to full strength. A few nights later, via computer, Bill verified the pattern over at least the last four years, and as much as he hated to accept the obvious, he realized recurring brief affairs were a way of life for Scott. He was shattered, and at the same time paralyzed by the insight. How could he share this with his sister? And yet how could he carry the burden himself? His mood, always one of introversion and isolation, became even more gloomy. For several weeks he bore the weight of this knowledge like a massive cross. Finally in desperation he sought consolation and in, of all places. an Episcopal confessional setting. The priest listened and told Bill what he thought he needed to hear. "This is a heavy trip and since it is weighing so heavily on your conscience. follow your conscience. Do what you feel you should do and since you've taken on a parental role for your sister. do what you think your parents would have done for her. I've been through this with others in similar situations. The wife is often the last to know and the result is often devastating. Follow your heart."

"Thank you. I guess that makes it pretty clear." Bill now felt quite relieved. since he had received permission to what he thought was right and proper in the first place. He had a plan.

A few days later. he invited Anne to join him for lunch at a new French restaurant on 51st Street. She had been somewhat surprised by his invitation. but he seemed so insistent. almost desperate, that she knew that something must be up. Throughout the meal. however. he spoke in platitudes. unrealistically recalling the ease of the old days until Anne found the whole situation tedious. Then. as they were on dessert and coffee he blurted out, "Your husband is having affairs." He was ill prepared for her response which was unremitting laughter.

"Well. of course he is." She finally had controlled her mirth. "Do you mean Ruth or all the others?"

Bill was astounded. He sat in dumbfounded silence as his sister explained. "If it doesn't bother me why should it upset you?" She resumed eating and went on to say that she was getting exactly what she wanted out of their relationship and she wasn't about to change. "Let's just talk about something else. something important, okay?" Bill was shocked into stupefaction by this attitude. His own sister! The mixture of chaotic emotions that this produced was something beyond him. Even the effect of their parents' sudden death paled in comparison.

CHAPTER 16

Certainly, the luncheon did nothing but worsen Bill's already dismal state of mind. Following the events of their meeting, he could scarcely think of anything else. Somehow he must do something, but what? In his despondent mood, his thinking was too impaired to be effective, so it wasn't until a chance event that he began to develop a plan that he felt might allow him some peace of mind. Ruth, whom he now considered to be second only to Scott in amoral standing, was ironically the one who presented it to him.

"Bill," she said to him one afternoon, "this U.S. Enterprises business we're doing to cover the Dallas Business Consortium; it's taking too much time and energy. There's got to be a simpler way to transfer funds out of TransNational Healthcare into U.S.E. on an automatic basis. My time, and my staff's talent, are being wasted, and when our stock splits, something has to be done or it will be even worse. Please make fixing this a high-priority over the next month. Scott and I both agree on the importance of this project, so get back to me with a solution."

I'll bet, how convenient, Bill thought to himself. Even so, he did appreciate that in some way this should present an opportunity. If it could be manipulated properly, it might be the vehicle to strike at both Scott and Ruth. He knew, however, that when all was said and done, Ruth was excellent at evaluating the impact of any financial transaction's smallest details, so any attempt to siphon off funds or subvert her orders would be extremely difficult to pull off. Still, he pondered a variety of tempting options.

Three weeks later, following one of the Sunday TransNational "prayer sessions," Bill offered Ron a ride home after the COO casually mentioned that his Jaguar had been acting up again and was in the shop. In actuality, Ron had come to suspect that all was not well with Scott and his brother-in-law, and his seemingly off-hand comment was made so that he could get Bill alone to assess the situation. Ron's wife and Anne were quite close and Anne had alluded, in an incidental remark, to the lunch that she and her "naive brother" had and commented on how upset Bill had been and how focused he had become on loathing Scott. Ron had immediately realized the potential opportunity. As they pulled out of the executive area of the basement office-building parking lot and headed up East Riverside Drive, he started his pitch. "You know Scott and I go way back, too," he began. "I think he's the most amazing businessman I've ever seen, but somehow he seems to be different recently. I guess there's a limit for all of us, in terms of what we can keep in our head."

"What do you mean *different?*" as Bill checked out the bait.

"Well, for me, I guess I'm not sure where I stand anymore. I can't seem to get things just right for him. I feel that my future here at TransNational is not as permanent as I'd hoped it would be. After we move to Little Rock next spring, I suspect I may be out on the street. I suppose I shouldn't be telling this to you, though; after all you guys are brothers." He lapsed into silence as Bill maneuvered the car into an express lane on the freeway which was moving more smoothly.

"Brothers-in-law are not the same as brothers, I can assure you," Bill finally answered. "I suspect that we're both considered dispensable by Scott. In fact, so is almost everyone in the organization, except Ruth, who may enjoy a special position."

"You mean on her back?" the Ron replied. He liked the way this was going.

"Well something like that. I don't know which way is really their favorite. After all you don't discuss the specifics of the talents of your brother-in-law's mistress with him." The anger in Bill's voice was now palpable.

Bull's eye, thought Ron, *now to close the deal.* "Well" he began, "I think Ruth may be on thin ice just like we probably are. Recently, when her name came up in a private conversation with Scott , he referred to her as a 'mercy fuck.' Wouldn't she love to hear that." He knew Bill would find satisfaction in this and most likely could be encouraged to use it sometime in the future. "Well we're about home," he went on. *He's taken the bait, now all I need to do is set the hook.* "How is the United States Enterprise money transfer project coming along?" he asked. They neared Ron's suburban driveway. He finished up by saying, "I guess the rich just get richer. Thanks for the ride. I appreciate it," and he exited the car well satisfied by the encounter. As he drove off, Bill also felt energized. *So Ruth is vulnerable too*, he smiled. If only he could figure out how to use the United States Enterprise project to do in Scott, but he was aware that the Dallas Business Consortium bean counters always ran on-line audits of all financial transfers, and the slightest discrepancy triggered an immediate inquiry and request for clarification/reconciliation. However, he had been raised by his grandmother, who taught the Presbyterian admonition that where there is a will there is a way.

Meanwhile there were a number of corporate projects, each of which increased the already monumental burden of managing TransNational Healthcare. The marketing department was in high gear and new subscribers, also known as "covered lives" were signing up in record numbers. They were attracted in some cases by the well-crafted advertising campaign, which was a daily staple of the television and newsprint media diet of those living in metropolitan centers. It targeted middle and upper-middle class employed populations in the 27-state market area, and was further promoted by the fact that human resources and benefits managers for many of the targeted large employers were encouraged to make TransNational their preferred health care program. This was done by simply offering TransNational Healthcare stock options as bonuses to those successful in steering the large numbers of their employees into TransNational programs. Sometimes, to make certain that there was no trail, these options were laundered through the families of the executives to obscure the transaction. These very same personnel managers could also ingratiate themselves to TransNational by pushing specific TransNational health insurance options, which had large upfront deductibles and co-payments once the deductibles had been met. These strategies were potent ways to decrease the number of doctor visits and at the same time, TransNational's costs of doing business. To handle the increased numbers of patients there was also, of course, still some need for the hospitals and clinics to deliver care. Fortunately, now that they were well known and had their reputation for toughness established, TransNational Healthcare take-over teams found bludgeoning these new providers into discounted payment rates to be easier than ever. The problems of reduced demand meant that doctors and hospitals were less busy and could be squeezed into taking lower reimbursement, since if they didn't sign the contract as written, a hungry competing hospital or doctor group would be more than willing to take it on, which again, increased TransNational's profit margin.

What was not so easy was to make sure that complaints by patients were kept to a minimum. It had always been Scott's established policy to focus on customer satisfaction. The *perception* of quality was all-important. He had figured out early on that his managers couldn't really determine quality health care, since they were non-healthcare professionals, so *appearance* became all-important. That would be preserved no matter what. Cutting corners on expertise or quality was an essential approach: always going with the lowest cost bidder for equipment, for example, but he always had lots of consumer advocates visible at all of his sites. These advocates were designated as patient representatives, and their job was to maintain client satisfaction, which Scott understood to be crucial for success. They were physically attractive young people with engaging personalities who exuded sincerity. They worked much cheaper than top-rank doctors and nurses, whose skills only made a difference in one or two cases per thousand anyhow. With respect to billing complaints, Scott knew that in more than eighty-five percent of cases where legitimate charges were denied by TransNational, patients wouldn't even contest the issue. They'd just pay out of their own pockets. As he'd learned during his apprenticeship at Hanrahan and Klein, this ratio applied to everything; from pediatric emergency room visits to bone marrow transplants. All of this was justified by TransNational under the rubric of making healthcare affordable.

The most attractive and profitable strategy for dominating the market, however, wasn't in reducing services, but in acquisitions. It was evident that big things could happen if the Clinton Healthcare Reform wasn't instituted. Currently there were just too many players among insurance companies to maintain profits long-term. The HMOs and hospital systems had proliferated virtually unchecked, so unless the market could be expanded, most of the available customers had already been recruited. The rest of the U.S. population was sticking to their current doctors and hospitals for their care and everyone was waiting to see what was going to happen. To further develop the size and scope of TransNational Healthcare, Scott knew of two very inviting targets; American Healthcare and Occidental Healthcare. If only he could acquire them, he would be covering forty-four states, all the ones with large markets, excluding only a few of the sparsely-populated Western areas. He could then truly realize his dream of dictating the face and form of health care in the entire U.S. Everyone would be forced to come to him.

His corporate headquarters, he had decided, would be in Little Rock, providing proof that the *local boy* really had made it good. It also kept him close to his sources of funding, not only Dallas but also to the Little Rock investment bankers who had emerged as such serious players. It had turned out that they were more than willing to bend the rules if the stakes were high enough and the risks of getting caught were suitably low. They were much more creative and hungry than their white-suited counterparts in Memphis. Finally, moving to Little Rock would get him out of New York City, which was too expensive, rigid, and conventional in thinking to suit him. And, anyway, New York was his wife's playground. He had not spent much time or effort in planning the TransNational Healthcare tower; his criteria had been quite simple. It must be over one hundred stories tall, and be striking in design like the Hancock Center in Chicago. His executive office and meeting rooms should be fully encased in glass so that surveillance could be carried out in every direction. He met once a month with the architects and engineers to make it clear that he was the client and if he liked it, it was good. If not, they were wrong. Fortunately, the senior partner of the architectural firm which was heading this project was a keen judge of human nature and had pegged Scott perfectly. He played directly to Scott's ego and narcissism and provided a design which captured the exact essence of what Scott represented. It was also a true masterpiece of modern design. A monument to Scott and TransNational Healthcare and a statement to show the world what corporate America could do in any industry, given the right opportunities and leadership. It was a mix of light-colored textured Tennessee limestone facings, the stone alternated with window glass to give a light and soaring presence. Scott was delighted, but insisted that his area must have a tight security system. As "emperor" in this day and age, one couldn't be too careful about keeping disgruntled kooks at bay. His requirements and criteria had been completely satisfied, however, and his oversight of the project had soon become much less intense. Although it was the talk of Little Rock, a fact which he enjoyed, he busied himself with other much more pressing issues, perhaps the most important being the opportunity to assure failure for government health care reform. As it evolved, the collapse arrived without much need for manipulation. The advertising campaign mounted by the small insurance companies had been effective, but it was the Republicans' sense, and the scent of blood, that really stopped the process. As the movement for

BS

reform of health care stalled and then imploded, and as the Republicans took over Congress, Scott moved into action in characteristic high velocity. He knew corporate interests would soon have the field to themselves without regulation or obligation. He saw the opening and went straight for it, abetted in no small measure by his leadership of the Western meeting a year earlier, where he'd established himself as a driver in the market and also a political seer, predicting as he did the demise of the Clinton plan. In the interim, Congress had evolved a strategy for encouraging Medicare enrollees to join prepaid care systems, which played directly into TransNational's hands. Using their sophisticated national marketing operation, Scott's organization went into a virtual feeding frenzy and was able to selectively recruit large numbers of basically healthy 65-year-olds. For this collection of healthy seniors, TransNational collected on average forty-eight hundred dollars a year, while spending an average of twelve hundred dollars, making this a most profitable line of business. Most of the unhealthy older patients were transferred into systems at the University medical centers, helping the rich get richer while adding to the deficits incurred by teaching hospitals.

Enabling all of this was the reality that, best of all, no restraining legislation had been passed by Congress, so Scott was free to expand TransNational Healthcare in his image, and that was exactly what he planned to do. Expansion via takeover of major competitors was a strategic challenge that Scott could now take on. He did in truth have the organization, the experience, the confidence and most of all the will to make this move. To embark on such an undertaking still presented formidable risks and barriers. First, there were the adversarial problems with the other CEOs. His brothers in the business of recasting healthcare knew, as did he, that they were into a good thing and they were not about to go quietly into the shadows of a forced retirement. In addition, there were the boards of directors of these rival corporations. Unlike TransNational healthcare which was basically Scott Richards Incorporated, his major competitors had involved advisory or oversight groups of powerful men who were leaders in their own fields of expertise. They collected large fees and stock options for their quarterly one day meetings where they enjoyed giving advice and counsel. Most of them flew into these gatherings in their private jets and such men were not about to let a business, in which they were organizationally and frequently financially invested, to be pilfered and see it pass quietly out of their control.

Consistent with the philosophy and approach he had developed, Scott had come to consider such obstacles simply as boosting the stakes of the contest and enhancing the elation of an eventual triumph. His opportunistic, aggressive and bold approach to such undertakings, perhaps originating in the genes acquired from his warrior ancestors, plus his intuition, made him an ideal leader for such assaults. In addition, his lieutenants beginning with Ron George, had all the proper talents and skills for carrying out such acquisitions. He knew he had the proper pieces in place to achieve the consolidation of the entire industry under his authority. First would be American Healthcare; he had already made contact with its CEO, John Moran at the Western Summit. American did have substantial market share, but Scott's information collected by George Whitney's well-placed moles indicated that it needed major restructuring and down-sizing if it was going to remain competitive. Occidental Healthcare was a perfect fit and was his second target, although unlike American, it was well run. It was, however, cash poor due to its rapid expansion and his intuition and killer instinct told him that it was, therefore, also vulnerable.

To begin the assault on American, he arranged "a chance meeting" with John Moran (not difficult since one of Moran's personal secretaries was also on the TransNational clandestine payroll) at a luxurious Cap-Ferrat resort on the French Riviera where Moran was staying with his wife. On this trip he had insisted that Anne accompany him. However, given the surroundings and ambiance she had to admit that this was not a physical hardship, and she was always good at keeping up appearances. Scott openly raised the question of a merger when the two couples were enjoying a degustation feast overlooking the Mediterranean. Moran's response had been just as Scott had hoped and expected, i.e., "Why should we, what's in it for American, and what's to my advantage?" Scott proceeded to demonstrate his detailed knowledge of the internal workings of American Healthcare down to such details as which departments were over-staffed and what projected cash flows were going to be available. He then launched into a discussion of what he estimated would be required in terms of a restructuring plan for American to remain competitive. His twenty-minute presentation left Moran figuratively open-mouthed and both wives bored. He realized that Scott almost knew more about his business than he did, and correctly surmised that his colleague must have been well informed by inside people at American. "Now to the question of why it is to your advantage," Scott resumed. "I'm sure that for an extremely knowledgeable and sophisticated person such as yourself, that's really a rhetorical question." He then outlined not a gold, but a platinum parachute, the profits of which had probably never been seen since the days of the robber barons. "Well, I'll have to think about that, I really just don't know . . . ," was Moran's reply. In reality, both he and Scott did know that the deal was done. All that remained was planning out the details and no small detail was avoiding the Securities Exchange Commission. Scott knew exactly which of his in-house lawyers should lead that project. As his 747 left Nice, he worked out details of the deal and as he touched down at Kennedy, he knew that this had been one of his most successful business trips ever, even if he did have to take his wife.

He had spent part of the flight reviewing his plans for the other takeover, Occidental Healthcare, and he soon found that as he had feared, this was going to be a difficult project. They had no interest in being merged or acquired, and they made their position known in response to the initial trial balloon floated their way. "Tell Mr. Richards that hell will freeze over before we will join with him," was their reply. Scott was neither surprised nor displeased since this represented now a real challenge, something he could appreciate for something he wanted to acquire. The ammunition for this battle would clearly be money. Scott planned to see to it that the Occidental Healthcare cash situation only got worse.

CHAPTER 17

The TransNational Healthcare tower was opened in Little Rock amid an avalanche of national attention and publicity. Scott had invited all the well-connected financial and political players in the South and Mid-Atlantic states to attend as his guests and hear what he modestly pronounced would be the most important speech of the decade on the subject of marketplace reform and health care delivery. He promised to provide a road map of a radically new and much improved system with industry standards to which he and the market could be held. His listeners were not to be disappointed. He gave them exactly what he had promised, as well as treating them to a celebration of corporate wealth which even by Little Rock's standards was quite opulent. Members of the Dallas Symphony provided the background as the guests arrived. The hors d'oveurs, champagne and catering had been imported from New York. Each guest received a crystal model of the TransNational Tower engraved with the date and a "thank you" signed by Scott. The dinner menu included Ostrich (very heart healthy), Beluga caviar and French Fois Grasse and truffles.

He predictably began his remarks by saying, "We dedicate this wonderful building to the principle of providing the health care that Americans want and deserve. The success of the affordable, quality service that TransNational Healthcare is giving to the country shows that we are the future of medical care. You can join us or be left behind. You can't replicate us, we've got too much of a head start. And you certainly can't fight us because we are too big and too good." This message was repeated directly and indirectly as he traced the swift rise of TransNational Healthcare and documented its now considerable assets. He conveniently omitted the facts that his organization did not support any care for those who could not pay, or that there was no budget for support of research or education or for development of new treatments of diseases such as AIDS or Alzheimer's. Publicly, of course, he pointed to his TransNational Healthcare charitable foundations which, in actuality, were efficiently fulfilling their mission, funneling assets back into the for-profit sector of the organization. He did, of course, dwell at length on the jobs he provided and the taxes he paid, even though most of the jobs had always been there before TransNational took over, and when TransNational reorganized the local system there were often simply fewer of them, especially the well-paying ones.

Missing from the audience were representatives of his competitors, for example, Occidental Healthcare and some old acquaintances such as Professor Rand and the management of Coastal Hospital and his original angel, Frank Powell, whose dissatisfaction was now virtually endless. Anne, who was constantly being bombarded by her brother to "wake up and nail the bastard," was unable to attend. A mysterious illness had struck and stranded her in New York City. She had sent her regrets. In spite of these notable absences, his remarks received wide publicity and enhanced the aura which he had carefully cultivated in hopes of making words become a reality. Scott felt that even his father, who had died five years earlier following heart surgery, could have approved of his son at this moment.

In spite of this, and unbeknownst to him, there were serious problems brewing in the upper tiers of his new tower. Bill had become fixated on how to bring Scott down. His obsessions had resulted in a remarkably simple plan, which was enthusiastically endorsed by his now co-conspirator, Ron George. They had developed a program that took advantage of the availability of U.S. Enterprise's dummy corporation. Each time there were financial transfers of profits to be laundered into U.S.E., there was a routine request for confirmation and sign off by an agent of the Dallas Business Consortium. The accompanying paperwork, which they had crafted, was a convoluted wordy electronic document which included a sentence which gave a waiver and transfer of stock voting rights to Ron George, as the Chief Operating Officer of TransNational. The Dallas Business Consortium accountants had no idea of what they were approving since they only looked at the money trail to see that the numbers balanced and not the fine print of the computer-generated checklist. As a result of this ploy, however, George was becoming a larger and larger proxy vote holder in TransNational Healthcare without spending a cent. This disarming ploy, of course, could not have taken place without the acquiescence of Ruth and given her involvement with Scott, this had presented a problem. It was however, not beyond the ability of the resourceful Ron. He casually shared with Ruth, Scott's "mercy fuck" remark which had been initially received by her with an immediate extraordinarily angry outburst directed towards the messenger, as well as frank disbelief. Ron's response which he had prepared in advance was, "Okay let's do a little experiment to show that I'm not the one that you should be abusing." He arranged a one-on-one session with Scott where the purpose was solely to get him to repeat himself. The difference was that this time Ruth was listening on an intercom. Playing on a mixture of his machismo and arrogance it had been no problem to get Scott to reproduce the epithet. Ruth was at first devastated. Although she still remained angry with Ron, her anger towards Scott had no limits. When Ron had seized the moment to outline what he and Bill wanted to do, she readily and enthusiastically pledged her assistance, making certain that these irregularities would never be called to Scott's attention so that the second phase of the plan could go forward.

THE LAST GRASP   **125**

Meanwhile, Scott had come to realize that one thing TransNational Healthcare needed was academic respectability. The acquisition of a medical school would provide this quite nicely and would also give TransNational Healthcare a site and systems for retraining his currently employed doctors and nurses into the TransNational mold. It would also provide a corps of newly graduated nurses and doctors, who through programs of tuition support and loans would be both indebted to, and ingrained with the business principles of the organization. His own medical farm team.

He set out to find a well-established reputed school which was having problems with the new financial realities of the health care environment. He thought that probably this would be a private school located in an urban setting where there would be a large burden of poor, Medicaid-type patients incapable of paying. One where the leadership didn't have the foresight or opportunity to expand into the suburbs where the well paying patients were. It should also be one where there was a relatively small component of central university support or inadequate endowment funds to continue on without experiencing severe fiscal problems. The search was easy. Eleven likely candidates were identified. Southeastern Medical School appeared an ideal target. It was in one of his primary service areas and was facing a huge shortfall in its annual budget. He also thought it would be especially sweet to confront his old adversary Dean White in a situation where the outcome was an assured victory. He booked the corporate jet for a flight to Charlotte. While in transit, he recalled that he had actually been invited six months earlier to speak to the Association of Medical School Deans. The title of his presentation was "How to prosper in the new Healthcare environment." Following his standard presentation (the same basic speech he had given at the TransNational tower dedication), he'd been pleased that a number of the deans in attendance had shown interest in holding discussions with him in the near future. Dean White of Southeastern, of course, had not been one of them. Scott felt confident about the outcome as he entered the office of the dean of Southeastern Medical School, and was smiling. When the meeting was over, he thought, White would be working for TransNational or he'd be unemployed.

White as a tall, angular, dark-haired New Englander had always seemed slightly out of place at Southeastern. He had, however, been highly successful in developing the research and educational aspects of the school since he had taken it over nine years earlier. At the present time, though, while the clinical and research activities were medical successes, cash flow and service reimbursement had declined giving him and his boss, the president of the university, considerable problems. Scott knew it, too.

"Dean White," Scott began, "at the risk of being trite let me say that I'm willing to let bygones be bygones and to try to help both of us. I want to have an integrated healthcare delivery system to increase my share of the market and I want access to the research and development capabilities of a prominent medical school such as your own. You need cash and a source of continuing financial support for the future, therefore, I think this is a win-win situation for both of us."

White realized that this was a formidable pitch, and was somewhat surprised as Scott went on to accurately describe the problems that White and Southeastern faced. As usual, Scott had done his homework.

"Okay," White asked, "suppose Southeastern accepts your offer of help, what are the strings? I want to hear the specifics of your requirements for us." Scott was waiting for exactly this question, which went directly to the heart of the issue.

"Well, I hope you'll think they are quite minimal. I want to designate some specific aspects of the clinical education curriculum, since we need to train the right kind of doctors. In addition I'd want to be sure that we would have seats at the table of the Board of Directors. Other than that all your researchers could do their thing, as long as funding for their grants keeps coming in. If they don't keep up, I could probably be able to kick in some research funding but I would want to designate their themes and areas of investigation. After all, if I'm paying the piper. . . ."

THE LAST GRASP 127

White was silent. *So that's it*, he thought, *of course we're into control.* He appreciated that if TransNational effectively regulated the education and research activities and could direct the Board of Trustees, his function as a medical school dean was virtually neutralized. "Mr. Richards," he said, "I'm impressed by your grasp of the business aspects of our school and that you know exactly how it would fit into your organization."

Scott smiled, "Thank you."

"But I wouldn't get into bed with TransNational Healthcare if my life depended on it. I know that my job is tenuous at present, but there are some things that are not negotiable and my self-respect is one of them. I know that I'm no match fiscally for you and your organization, since the saying on the street is that there isn't enough shark repellent in the world to permit anyone to even get into a swimming pool with you. However, I wouldn't sell out the faculty and the patients that we serve for the twelve million pieces of silver or anything else you have to offer. Good afternoon."

Scott was still smiling as he left. A few phone calls to contacts at the university's Board of Directors, a leaked fax of a copy of the TransNational proposal for the Southeastern Med. bailout plan and a planted series of articles in the local newspaper about "Problems at Southeastern Medical School" soon resulted in a summons that found Dean White in the University President's office. Following an intense meeting between the two of them, a memo appeared in all Medical School faculty members' mailboxes, and on their e-mail, stating that the President had accepted with regret the resignation of Dean White. A few weeks later, the President was pleased to report to the Board of Trustees and the Alumni, "A landmark partnership with TransNational Healthcare." The newly appointed Dean and Scott and the President were photographed in congenial poses as the legal documents were initiated in the dean's office. Not surprisingly, the faculty underwent a dramatic change in the next few months. A majority of the researchers whom Dean White had recruited left. And the new dean unveiled a strategy for Southeastern of "Training primary care health care providers for the next century." At the same time, he announced a tuition-support plan and said the previous fiscal problems at Southeastern Med. had been resolved and fiscal health had been restored thanks to a trust fund generously supplied by TransNational Healthcare. This fund, of course, was a tax deduction for TransNational Healthcare and had the details of Scott's conversation with ex-Dean White been known to the IRS, inurnment for TransNational would have been fairly easy to prove. As it was, Scott and his organization seemed to have just acquired another prestigious shiny trophy.

CHAPTER 18

Back in Texas, Frank Powell's final estrangement from Scott Richards came abruptly and was the result of a family affair. It began with Elaine Powell, a distant niece, who had always been a favorite with him because of her delightful personality. Bright, energetic and attractive she'd been an example of the classic blond college cheerleader at Texas Christian University and after graduation had married her college sweetheart, Charlie Thompson, the captain of the golf team. Charlie who looked and sometimes played like Jack Nicklaus had worked and played well enough to become a mid-level executive in a small independent west Texas oil company. They had two children and life was good for this all-American couple. That is until when, at age 38, she was diagnosed with breast cancer. Initially everything seemed to the Thompsons to be going well. The surgery was not terribly disfiguring and was completed without complications. The follow-up radiation treatments which the doctors had recommended "just to make sure" had not made her sick at all. It always seemed during her visits however, that her doctors were constantly concerned about the future and they never really said that things were "all right"; they just told her to keep coming back. A year and a half after the operation they informed her in a manner that seemed especially ominous, that she needed some more tests and that she should come back so they could talk some more, in a week or so. The Thompsons and the oncologist, Dr. Joe Davidson, who had a sad Lincolnesque demeanor and appearance, looked equally grim when they faced each other in the consulting room one week later.

"The news is not good, we're so sorry." Dr. Davidson began, looking even more dour than usual. "We can give you a course of chemotherapy but we've scanned the material in the data bank registry and by far the best and most realistic chance for a cure for you at this point is a bone marrow transplant, which would be a rough few months but would give you odds of 2 out of 3 for a total cure; while, the chemo for a cure: well, it's about like winning the lottery 'tho it would probably buy some time." The Thompsons looked at each other and nodded. "There's no real choice is there? When can we start the transplant?" was Elaine's response.

"Probably in about two weeks. I'll call your insurance company for approval and our nurse practitioner will be in touch with you in the next several days to start the pre-transplant medication program. The sooner the better at this point."

But it wasn't the nurse who called, it was Dr. Davidson. "We've got a big problem." he said. "The insurance company won't cover a transplant; they say it's experimental and anyhow given the poor outlook of your type of tumor, they think it's not a good investment. Besides, they say that according to our contract we weren't even supposed to discuss it with you without their prior permission."

To Elaine and Charlie these stunning words sounded like a death sentence. "What can be done?" she finally sighed.

"I've already faxed an appeal to their chief medical director with the data from the National Tumor Bank Registry, and I'll push to get an answer, although the companies usually drag their feet. We'll hold off on the chemo for now since you feel well, at least physically." was Davidson's reply.

THE LAST GRASP

BS

He was all too accurate; in spite of e-mail messages and phone queries it took nine weeks and the final answer confirmed their initial negative response, although of course "Regretfully." The Thompsons sat in their living room that night after the children were in bed, and cried. Hers were tears of disappointment anxiety and fear, his of rage and frustration with anger that was palpable. He finally spoke, "I'm calling the local TV station, they're always doing health related stories, and this one's a beaut." It worked. The next evening a filming crew spent an hour with them eliciting the story, catching the tears and angst on their tape.

"It'll air tomorrow night," was the reporter's parting word. It did, although the story was edited down to a 2 minute, 39 second bite which included a statement from a TransTexas Health Care spokeswoman of "no comment," except that "this is standard company policy with respect to unproven, risky and experimental treatments."

The viewing audience included several interested parties besides the Thompsons. Dr. Davidson exploded in fury, "Unproven, risky, experimental, bullshit! Those people are not only thieving criminals, they're liars, look at the data from the protocols, you Philistines," was his passionate assessment and reply to the TV screen which paradoxically was now running a marketing advertising spot for TransTexas Healthcare. Another somewhat unanticipated viewer was Frank Powell, whose local station had picked up the story as a human interest "filler." Like Davidson he couldn't believe it either but for different reasons.

"That's my niece and one of my investments," was his shocked response. He made two quick phone calls. One to Elaine assuring her that he'd "fix this tonight," and "how sorry he was that he hadn't heard earlier" and finally "not to worry." When he hung up there were more tears from Elaine, but these were of course tears of joy, the first hopeful relief that they'd had in several months. Powell's second call was to Scott Richards and its result was not quite so satisfactory.

"I'll look into it first thing in the morning," was Richards' smooth, soothing reply, 'tho with more than a hint of irritation. Just what he needed was this kind of micro-meddling, "why doesn't he mind his own business!" Scott did perfunctorily check with his Dr. Johnson, who was still his willing servant and medical director, to be sure that all the legalities were covered with respect to proper documentation and then he called Powell.

"I really am sorry," he began, "but this is the only way to handle this problem. If we make an exception we'd eventually have to do all of them and we're talking up to a half to three quarters of a million each. I'm sure you understand that this is strictly business."

"No, I sure as hell can't. You're telling her to go crawl into a hole and die," was the response.

"Not at all, there are other treatments. There's chemotherapy, for example."

"Her docs say that in her case that's a 1:100 shot. This stinks and I won't have any part of it."

"Suit yourself," and the phone line went dead in Powell's ear.

A call to Elaine followed. "I'm taking care of this, get your bag packed." Next Powell called Doctor Davidson who was in the midst of his daily dictations when his answering service called with the announcement that Frank Powell, whom the operator knew to be one of the richest men in Texas, was on the phone and had said that he had a solution for the life and death problems of Mrs. Thompson and that they had to talk.

"Where's the best place in the country for her to go and get a transplant?" was the way he began the conversation. "Seattle," was the immediate reply. "I trained there, they've got the most experience and I know them personally."

"Fine, get her records, please call them and we're on our way. Money is no issue I've got it and I'm spending it." The call to Seattle was one that Davidson was glad to make and 36 hours later, thanks to Frank Powell's private jet and Dr. Davidson's calls, the Thompsons were in the appropriately sterile environment of the University of Washington, Oncology Center building. Ten days later the bone marrow transplant was successfully completed. Powell returned home but not before leaving a $250,000 check. "When this runs out, please send me an itemized statement and I'll write another" was his parting instruction to the billing office. When he got back to Texas he knew full well that he had something else to do; a personal call upon Scott Richards. The CEO's secretary tried to put him off, having been fore-warned that Powell would likely show up. He'd have none of it.

"Don't worry," he assured her, "it won't be a long visit, but he's going to see me." "Richards," he began taking charge of the meeting as he burst in, "For giving you your start I'll probably rot in hell. The only consolation is you'll be there, too. I'm done with you and TransNational Health Care. I sold all my stock over the past two weeks and I feel clean, something you don't understand since your only real emotional attachment is to the bottom line."

"Well, my sanctimonious ex-partner, as you Texans say, 'adios mother-fucker.' For a brief period you and your money were helpful but since that first year you've been excess baggage. I knew you were selling off, the comptroller's office was tracking it and we reconciled your dumping by doing some reciprocal trading so we actually advantaged our fiscal posture. Thanks for a last bit of help and now get the hell out of here before I get you thrown out."

Never one to miss the last word, Powell leaned forward as he rose from his chair, "What goes around comes around, Richards, and you and I are not over. If you think we are, you still don't understand Texas." He flung the door open as he exited the office making no attempt to close it. Richards' ever efficient executive assistant quietly shut it a few moments later.

The news from Seattle, unfortunately, was not encouraging. Due to the three month delay the transplant oncology team had not been able to use their optimum program and infections had become a major complication. One resistant germ after another attacked Elaine's weakened body, pneumonias and blood stream infections came in succession, resulting in what seemed to be a never ending litany of bad reports. She ranged between delirium and coma for days until a final meningitis due to a bacteria, with an unpronounceable name, unresponsive to all known antibiot-ics, became her immediate cause of death.

"We're so very sorry. Try to remember the good times and take care of your family. You've got great kids and a great supporter in Frank Powell. We'll let him know how she gave it a great try. Guts just weren't enough," intoned the lead oncologist as he and the bereavement group members tried to console the seemingly inconsolable and despondent widower who sat immobilized at his wife's now darkened bedside in the intensive care unit. The intravenous lines had been pulled out and the monitors and the respirator were now silent as the team withdrew to let him say his last good-byes.

"The *Moraxella catarrhalis* organism was just the last straw. What really did it was the prolonged delay in initiating the transplant. That really stacked the deck against her. What I'd like to put on the death certificate is not breast cancer and meningitis but murder by an insurance company," the lead oncologist subsequently railed to his colleagues. "It's all so tragic for the patients. We doctors and the hospitals will somehow adapt to survive and be okay in this new order, but the whole system is being destroyed, disappearing before our very eyes, bastardized by the bean counting bastards. We can't seem to do a thing about it. I sure wish the Clintons or somebody had derailed this whole business before it got up so much momentum."

As he had so often done in the past, Frank Powell had evolved a more direct plan than that of just wishing.

BS

CHAPTER 19

Following his resignation from Southeastern, Richard White received numerous job offers, especially as the facts of the matter came to light. His unwillingness to compromise his principles, and his spirited defense of the medical school faculty and the indigent patients being served at his institution, became common knowledge within the medical community in a matter of weeks. It was, of course, the material of which legends were made. He was offered leadership positions with private philanthropic agencies and medical think tanks, deanships at several prestigious universities, and medical directorships at institutions that many of his contemporaries would have killed for. Many of these positions would have doubled or tripled his previous Southeastern salary. However, when he found that his old position at Metro had become vacant, his re-entry to that setting was completed in short order. His triumphant return was followed by a period of professional equanimity such as few men are fortunate enough to experience.

A few months later, however, he was somewhat perplexed when a Mr. Frank Powell appeared on his appointment calendar. He was told by his secretary that this was a meeting arranged at Mr. Powell's request by the fundraising office of the hospital, who had confirmed that Mr. Frank Powell was indeed very wealthy.

"Good day. What can I do for you? I don't believe we've ever met." Dr. White greeted his visitor.

"No, Dr. White, we've only interacted indirectly. I'm the Judas who gave Scott Richards his start and although it made me even richer than I was before, I still feel quite guilty. In particular, I've heard what happened to you, and I'm blaming myself for your dismissal." He went on to give a brief background of County Healthcare Network, TransTexas Healthcare, and his falling out with Scott Richards.

"Well, Mr. Powell, I guess I understand why you came to visit, but at this time I'm firmly convinced that what happened turned out to do me a great personal favor. I've never been happier nor felt more productive. No hard feelings, you have no need to feel blame on my account."

"I'm glad to hear that, of course," Powell said. "But I didn't come here to receive an absolution. I've investigated you and I want you to know that I've set aside ten million dollars in a fund to be put at your personal disposal. It's administered through the 4th National Bank of Texas in Houston, and it's for you to use as you see fit. You're the sole trustee. If you don't use it, the interest just accrues. I believe in investing in people, and apparently you do too. I can't think of a better way to assuage my guilt in all that's happened, than to give someone like you the ammunition to use when the time is ripe."

For once, Dr. White was completely taken aback. "I don't know what to say except thank you," he said.

"That's more than enough. My legal staff will send you the details. I hope we meet again sometime soon to savor success in dealing with the Scott Richards' of the world. Until then, adios." With that, he excused himself, leaving his host to muse about the sometimes peculiar and perverse way the world worked.

CHAPTER 20

The planning of the acquisition-merger of American Healthcare was highly technical and since it would significantly increase TransNational Healthcare activities and market share, it was crucial that the government be kept at bay in terms of anti-trust issues. In view of his successes with TransTexas, Ken Franklin had been given the key job of setting the paperwork up so that it would clear the Justice Department's hurdles. He was a serious young man, proud of his professional skills and was initially quite pleased to be given this large responsibility. As he began to delve into the specifics of his assignment, however, he came to appreciate its complexity. His weekly meetings with Chief Counsel Joe Thomas were helpful with the technical fine points, and by spending eighteen-hour days and meeting repeatedly with his counterparts at American Healthcare, he had created a tight case for a TransNational Healthcare takeover.

"A masterpiece!" was the verdict of his mentor. "Mr. Richards will love it, I know. And you should be elated as well."

Ken, however, looked worried. "What do you think are the long-term implications for American?" he asked. "Some of those guys seem awfully nervous about job security. Especially given Mr. Richards' reputation as a cost-cutter and downsizer."

"Tell them not to worry. It's going to be business as usual for all of 'um," Thomas said. "Mr. Richards says so."

Richards in his discussions with Thomas and the other members of the senior management group had, of course, outlined just the opposite strategy. He planned a rapid downsizing of American, retaining only those essential employees in the most productive divisions. Most of those who were invited to stay would do so at a reduced salary. Scott's final admonition to his inner circle of senior managers, including Joe Thomas, had been, "reassure them that nothing will change and figure that seventy-five percent will be out in six months." No one in the room at that time doubted that he meant it. Thomas, however, correctly felt that his sensitive junior associate would find this approach very troublesome and therefore had presented to him the contrary reassuring scenario. At the conclusion of their meeting, Ken did indeed seem comfortable as he left and was truly relieved by his boss' reassurance. As he walked back to his office he had no true appreciation of the ultimate significance of this project and in particular, he could not imagine how it would affect him personally.

The plan for the Occidental Healthcare takeover was an entirely different affair. Internal espionage and secrecy were the order of the day. The strategy worked. "Boss, I've got it all," was the enthusiastic pronouncement of George Whitney. "Their sources of cash, the confidential log-on into their computer so we have access to their on-line profit and loss spread sheet, the specifics of the performance of each of their practice sites, their moment-to-moment cash flow, and their projected budget plans and strategies, I've got it all." He went on. "They are very vulnerable. They've over-extended something fierce. But if they get financing in twelve to fifteen months," he added, "they'll be on a solid basis and will be a challenge anywhere our businesses overlap. "Also," he added, "their strategic plan is almost as aggressive as ours."

"Nice job, George. I'll see that they don't get that funding. That's the next task. Looking at what you've given me, it should be quite feasible. Let's obtain a list of their potential credit sources, and I'll explore freezing them out."

Scott Richards began telephoning and found his first call reassuring. It was to the CEO of a major banking chain with whom Scott had a current nine-digit line of credit which could be activated with an electronic transfer on a moment's notice. "Hello, Fred. I just wanted to let you know 'bout our expansion plans since we expect to use your generous offer of help," Scott went on to review his plan for growth. This was his thinly disguised way of promising business and helping a friendly investor by spreading his insider information with respect to stock issues and options. "By the way, it would be a real favor to me if you would be prudent in approving any transfers to competitors; Occidental Healthcare, for example. If that didn't happen, it would be worth a lot in points the next time we negotiate. How's the family?"

Fred countered, "All is well."

"Good. Hope to see you soon, nice talking with ya. Bye." *Very good*, he thought to himself as he contemplated the exchange. *If the next dozen calls go well, we will have the trap set and sprung.* He then moved on to the misinformation piece, planting rumors and stories of "problems at Occidental." After that, all that was needed was a gentle push and the fatal avalanche would start, soon developing a life of its own.

CHAPTER 21

As contemplations faded from his consciousness. Scott thought to himself. *Yes. it's been a very long time coming.* He was already savoring. with enormous satisfaction. the forthcoming annual meeting. He stood in his tower watching the sun disappear over the low Arkansas hills. knowing that Occidental Healthcare lay almost defenseless for his taking. He'd sent them an offer outlining the conditions which effectively amounted to a surrender: in return he would transfer the cash that they required to at least make payroll. The deadline for the response was midnight prior to the TransNational Healthcare annual meeting. and Scott was certain it would be positive. He felt omnipotence within his grasp. His vision of himself as the health czar of the country was just over the horizon.

The meeting itself should be a huge success. just with the announcement of the American merger alone. He'd gone over every detail of the strategic plan for the upcoming year which would be outlined tomorrow. It now included the takeover of Occidental Healthcare and the effective domination of the market. The keynote speech at the end of the meeting would be delivered by a respected former Secretary of the Treasury, who would canonize Scott and TransNational Healthcare as saviors, restoring sanity and responsibility to the system. He'd describe them as an example of how the American marketplace had triumphed over governmental bureaucracy. It was remarkable how fifty thousand dollars for an hour's speech changes one's perspective. Scott then actually planned a brief vacation and celebration returning to Cap-Ferrat for a few days. This time, his companion wouldn't be his wife, although Anne was expected to keep up appearances and attend the annual meeting.

The next morning Scott walked briskly across the tarmac with his characteristically determined style, and with his usual aggressive stance brushed aside local reporters who wanted to ask about the recent death of Ken and "the personal problems surrounding it."

"It certainly had nothing to do with his work," he told the press. "which I guess was apparently the only good thing about his life. You'll really have to talk to our security group, I'm on my way to New York City." With that brusque comment, he ascended into the TransNational jet.

Actually, Ken had done quite well with the technical-legal parts of the American merger. His politically conservative background made him very comfortable doing battle with a regulatory branch of the government, such as the Securities Exchange Commission. Scott had appreciated early on that this young lawyer was very good at what he did, both conceptually and technically, and the idea of harnessing him to this project was basically just good management. His documents were always meticulous and articulate. The character trait that had led to his suicide, of course, was his conscience. Along with his conservative politics, he was deeply religious and, after his reassuring conversations with his boss he had somehow envisioned a TransNational Healthcare merger which was consistent with the innocent picture of the deal that the public relations department promoted. "A public service system bringing affordable, quality health care to America." Throughout his career he had used his conservative orientation and religious faith to maintain a naive belief system, attributing goodness to others where it clearly did not exist, rationalizing away and justifying any cognitively dissonant aspects in his daily life, including his work at TransNational. The final agreement for American, however, ultimately caused him to face the reality that was to result in his destruction. At the monthly meeting of the five lawyer senior counsel group, of which he was now a full member, he had opened by briefly reviewing his finalized merger document. At the conclusion of his presentation, his peers were congratulatory, high praise from some of the best and most highly paid talent in the health law business. Legal coverage was one area where Scott didn't cut corners.

"Before we move on, Ken, how much do you estimate this will save TransNational on the American consortium balance sheet?" asked one of those present.

Ken replied, "I doubt it will save very much, since both organizations already use such things as group purchasing and economies of scale."

"No, I mean with respect to down-sizing of American personnel," the questioner persisted.

"I don't believe there will be much reduction except for the top executives with parachutes. That's how Mr. Richards explained it," Ken answered. The response of the other members of the team was an unrestrained roar of laughter. It seemed to be amplified as it resounded off the hardwoods of the teak and mahogany walls and furniture of the room. "What's so funny?" Ken asked.

"Well, since you asked, I guess it's time I told you," replied Chief Counsel Thomas as he pulled out a thick-bound tract marked confidential with a bright red border. "Here's our plan: A minimum of seventy percent reduction of American personnel within one year; we get their facilities, keep a few of their technical and medical personnel whom we really need; the rest are out. And best of all since their jobs don't exist anymore our exposure under current tax and liability regulations is minimized. It's a ten billion dollar a year deal. Great job, Ken."

Ken was stunned. Somehow he'd actually believed that this was just a simple expansion of his parent organization. The idea of costing thousands of fellow human beings their livelihood never even occurred to him after his early conversations. And at a time that jobs in the medical field were becoming scarce! He was numb and dazed. He remembered nothing of the rest of the five-hour session. When it was over, he asked to meet Thomas. "Is it really true? Are all those people really to be cut out? Please tell me you were exaggerating the effects."

His boss was tired and had a headache which had begun after a huge fight that morning at breakfast with his wife and teenage son. At this moment, he was not a happy man. "Hell son, grow up, that's the name of the merger game. Get the factory and unload the workers."

Ken didn't remember anything about the drive home. When he arrived he sat for several hours in a state of paralyzing shock staring out into the night. It seemed to him that his life had lost its meaning and that he had participated in an act so atrocious that it could never be atoned. He thought perhaps he could talk it over with someone else, maybe Reverend Smith, the pastor of his Christian church. Yes, that was it. He wanted to be told that it really would somehow be okay. He dialed the cleric's home number which rang once, twice, three times without a response. After twenty rings he reluctantly hung up. What he hadn't remembered in his despondency was that the Smith family was on spring vacation in the Florida Panhandle. The church bulletin last week had said to call the associate pastor for any emergencies, and for some reason his call had not triggered the automatic call forwarding device. In his despondent stupor, he impulsively concluded that he knew how he could fix it and make things all right. He calmly went to the closet, loaded his hunting rifle and ended his psychic pain simply by pulling the trigger. The cleaning woman found him sprawled on the floor. The note she found said only *Forgive me.* The gun muzzle had fallen against the window sill and by chance pointed directly at the pyramidal cupola at the summit of the TransNational tower.

The TransNational limo was waiting at the private terminal at LaGuardia as Scott's plane touched down and he curtly acknowledged his two colleagues as he entered the vehicle and they sped off towards Manhattan. As he, Ron and Ruth reviewed the annual meeting agenda and the damage control for Ken's suicide, which apparently was not going to be a problem for Moran or American, his mood was for him, almost jovial. The planning session continued when they reached the hotel where a faxed copy of the capitulation of Occidental was handed to Scott by the Assistant Hotel Manager. Scott accepted it with a fleeting moment of joy and reconvened the meeting with Ruth and Ron. Finally at midnight, when he felt nothing was left to chance, they adjourned to reassemble in the morning, a half hour before the opening of the annual session.

For Scott this was it. The long awaited reward of all the years of planning and work which would literally be crowned by the successful outcome of the shareholders meeting. He was certainly not a man given easily to enjoyment or even contentment, however, at this moment he felt the very human emotions of exhilaration mixed with a gleeful anticipation. He would have mastery over the entire industry, since he would literally be in personal control of over one-half of it; he would call the tune. It was all within his grasp. He had vanquished his enemies from the field: the competing CEOs, the doctors like that obnoxious White, the holier than thou reformers and all the others who had given him trouble along the way.

Too bad they couldn't all be present to watch, he mused. At this moment, when he felt invincible, his usually perceptive intuitions gave him no premonitions of the possible insecurity of his grip upon forthcoming events. His defenses were temporarily lowered.

CHAPTER 21

The shareholders meeting was to take place in the glassed and mirrored grand ball room of the Hilton. A stage had been erected at one end with an assortment of large and small chairs to accommodate the various major players. A large podium dominated the center of the dais. Off to the left was a large electronic scoreboard to record the proxy votes on the various upcoming agenda items.

The meeting began on-track and on-schedule. After Ruth's presentation of the spectacular financial year that TransNational had enjoyed, she announced a forthcoming stock split which would be worth at least a hundred and fifty dollars per share. TransNational had, once again, emerged as the darling of Wall Street, due among other things to rumors of big new mergers in the offing. The vast majority of mutual fund managers already looked upon it with great favor even though it was currently selling on the New York Stock Exchange in the hundred and sixty dollar a share range. A thunderous round of applause gave approbation to her remarks. Scott beamed. After a few perfunctory questions, Scott was introduced with the dry comment that he had a few announcements to make.

Scott began, "I know that all of you are delighted about the merger with American. I'd like you all to acknowledge my good friend, colleague and new partner, Charlie Moran. Stand up Charlie." Moran did so on cue and polite applause was his reward. "What I now want to talk about is something that gives me similar pleasure, and I know it will excite all of you as well. Let me simply tell you that Occidental Healthcare has agreed to become a wholly owned subsidiary of TransNational Healthcare. Copies of the letter of intent are being distributed by the staff members who are proceeding down the aisles." As he spoke, a cadre of young people in blazers with the TransNational Healthcare logo emblazoned on the breast pocket materialized into the aisles and distributed the Occidental Healthcare capitulation papers. Pandemonium ensued. Nearly every trader in the room reached for his or her cellular phone to call in a major buy-order for TransNational. The volume of applause and cheers were like the din more often heard in Madison Square Garden than at staid stockholders' meetings. Scott gloried in this, his moment. "I guess you like this almost as much as I did," was his wry remark. After making a few projections about his personal visions for the future, he returned to his chair, which not surprisingly was situated center stage and was larger, higher and more formal than those occupied by other members of the stage party.

Now, only a few perfunctory agenda items and then the concluding keynote address. The meeting was being chaired by Charles Bell as Chairman of the Board of TransNational Healthcare. Only a few of those in attendance appreciated the subtle fact that he was also the recent head of the Dallas Business Consortium and those who knew were not about to make that connection public.

"Next, we have the voting, although after these reports, I guess the result won't be in doubt, will it?" Bell said. The standing Board of Directors was confirmed by a hundred and thirty three thousand to less than one thousand votes. "There're always a few crackpots and cranks," he remarked to Scott who was seated next to him. Ruth and Ron were confirmed by similar margins as the temporary electronic scoreboard registered the vote.

"Now for the president and CEO, I would think this would be unanimous," Bell said as he gave the signal for the tally. "Scott Richards; fifty-nine thousand one hundred and thirty-seven, Ron George; seventy-four thousand nine hundred and seventy-three" read the board. The room which had been rocked with noise a few minutes ago was as silent as a tomb. Scott momentarily sat red-faced and immobile and then exploded.

"What the hell is going on here? Is this some kind of a bad joke?" His comment was picked up by the P.A. system, not that he cared.

"Well, it just looks to me that you're out of a job now," replied Ron George calmly. Ruth was sitting next to him, smiling broadly. The previously unflappable Chairman of the Board, who had been conducting the well-oiled meeting seemed dumbfounded by this turn of events and sat silent and motionless.

Ron George strode to the podium. "Ladies and gentleman, for clarification, I've just voted seventy-three thousand eight hundred and eleven proxies, which have accrued to me, by the fact that agents, for a number of the major stock holders have signed over to me the voting rights of their stock shares." He then projected a series of slides highlighting the portions of the documents which had been routinely signed by the Dallas Business Consortium designees as part of the money laundering scheme, giving him the Consortium's proxy votes. He also gave a copy to the TransNational Healthcare Chief Counsel seated to the right of Ruth on the stage. "Any questions, ahhhh?"

A low level of conversation was now audible everywhere throughout the room. Those traders who had recently placed TransNational buy-orders were now back on their cellular phones with stop-orders. Everyone in the crowd, it seemed, was conferring with their neighbors about this stunning and unprecedented turn of events. Richards sprang from his seat to consult chief counsel Thomas, who looked grim. Ron George walked over and handed Scott another copy of the transfer of proxy agreements. "I 'd hate to have you look over his shoulder, here's your own personal copy. You can read it at your leisure, in your retirement. You'll find it iron-clad. You've got twenty-four hours to clear out of the office. I'm in charge now and I promise there will be some major changes made." He turned to the Chair of the meeting and said, "Mr. Bell, I've taken the liberty of bringing a copy of the articles of incorporation for you. You'll notice that I am indeed in charge. You see, Mr. Richards had them set up so that you and the Board have no real opportunity to meddle with top management or second guess their say. Since I'm in charge now, I say that we adjourn."

By now, word about the dramatic events at the TransNational meeting was on the street and reporters and photographers suddenly materialized on the scene and were busily snapping pictures non-stop and trying to get statements from any of the participants, since they appreciated that this was probably the biggest business story of the year. On the stage and in the meeting room, turmoil seemed to have become the order of the day. "Adjourn the meeting now," Ron said. Chuck Bell looked at the TransNational Chief Counsel for advice. He nodded acquiescence. Bell brought the events to conclusion by intoning, "I declare this stock holders' meeting adjourned!"

Scott had recovered and was starting to function. "You bastards can't get away with this. I'll have your balls nailed to the wall before sunset." He faced Bill and Ruth.

"Mine too?" Ruth smiled as she joined in. "No more mercy fucking, eh, Scott? Since time is running out on your twenty-four hours, I suggest you get the hell out to LaGuardia A.S.A.P. Since the TransNational limo and jet are no longer available to you, a cab and a commercial jet will make it a longer and somewhat different trip back to Little Rock than what you enjoyed on the way out. I am sure it would be a pleasure to see security toss you out of the tower on your royal ass. That will occur exactly twenty-three hours and twenty-two minutes from now if you're not out of your former office."

"We'll see whose vital parts are in jeopardy, my friends." And with that threat, Scott turned and still in character, swaggered off the stage. In the third row, Bill Winter sat smiling a very broad grin as he watched his sister, who remained motionless with a bewildered look upon her face.

THE LAST GRASP 149

As he left the hotel, reporters swirled about him. "Mr. Richards! Mr. Richards! Mr. Richards!" was their cry, as the television cameras ground on and microphones were thrust into his face. Finally, Scott reached his commandeered rental limo and turned to them snarling, "I'll give you what you want. A statement that is also a prophecy. When this affair is all over, there'll only be one of us left standing and if it isn't me then the whole temple will have come crashing down on them, and my friends, you can bet on it. They think this is a defining moment; well they're dead wrong. This is just the beginning." With that, he slid into the limo and was gone, on his way to the private aviation area of the Newark airport. He had already, by phone, engaged a private jet to fly to Little Rock. He charged it, of course, to the TransNational Healthcare account. Since the air-service scheduling secretary had not yet seen any TV news, that at least, had not been a problem. He'd started planning for his counter offensive as the limo sped through the Holland Tunnel. He knew he needed legal counsel since he would be mounting a challenge the likes of which they'd never seen, but most of all he needed financial backing. A huge line of credit, big enough that he might not even have to draw on it, but with its availability and implied muscle he believed he could mount a campaign that would quite likely be enough to panic most of the coup supporters into total retreat. With his connections, he reasoned, that shouldn't be hard to organize. He sat upright in the sedan, looking like a tightly coiled wire, while composing his list of calls. He took it for granted that the Dallas Business Consortium group would give him a running start which would probably be all that he'd need to deal with these back-stabbers. He still didn't see how they had gotten as far as they had with their intrigues and machinations. It never occurred to him to consider that they had been trained by a world class expert.

The limo came to a stop and Scott sprang from the vehicle throwing a skimpy tip in the direction of the driver. He took off in a trot towards the number three hanger where his plane was supposed to be waiting. A young uniformed cabin attendant was there, but no plane.

"Mr. Scott?" the twenty-three-year-old began.

"You're goddamn right that's who I am and I want to know where the hell my plane is. What kind of an incompetent operation are you people running? I want it here now." His face was nearly purple. This was truly the last goddamn straw.

"Mr. Scott, there's been a problem with the financial arrangements. I'm afraid the charge wasn't approved," the attendant responded calmly.

"Jesus Christ," exploded Scott, as he ripped the nearby phone receiver out of its cradle. "I want to talk to the president of this Mickey Mouse club now!"

"President Smith isn't in, but the operations officer, Mr. Perkins, will speak with you now, Mr. Scott," came the soft reply from the service operator. They had been expecting his call.

"Perkins here."

"Listen, you pygmy," Richards roared into the phone, "what's this about the payment arrangements for my trip to Little Rock?"

"Well, Mr. Richards, it seems that the TransNational Healthcare accounting office refused approval of your reservation. They said you were on your own since your corporate charge code has been canceled by Ms. Bonner."

Fifty minutes later, still seething from having had to use a personal account, he was airborne and began making his calls. The first one was to Tom Winston, the current President of the Dallas Business Consortium.

"Mr. Winston is in conference at the present time," came the reply in a slow Texan drawl.

"Well, young lady, you'd better tell him that this is Scott Richards and he'll take the call."

"One moment, please." Thirty seconds later she returned on the line. "He said that he'd get back to you. Please give me the number where you'll be in the morning, so that he can call you back."

"The morning, bullshit. Put me through to Sloan." Maybe at least the executive vice-president hasn't lost his mind. The call forwarding took only a moment. "Sloan, what the hell is with the group there? We need to get into high gear and go after those three bastards."

"Where are you? On Mars? Don't you know what's happened?" Sloan's voice came on. "Trading in your stock has been suspended by the New York stock exchange since TransNational went from a hundred and sixty three to a hundred and twenty three. That's a one day loss of more than 25% and triggers a three-day automatic suspension. The group here is meeting at this moment and strategizing how to cut their losses and get out!"

"Get out! Get out? This is the time to buy and drive all of those spineless wonders from the field."

"Richards, (no longer Scott or even Mr. Richards) you don't get it. They are getting out. They figure you have already cost them over six billion and counting; they're moving on."

Well, damn those gutless wimps, thought Scott after he'd hung up. Yet he was uncharacteristically dismayed by the conversation, and his usually focused, thoughtful and concentrated demeanor was disrupted to the point that he found himself unable to prioritize his next moves, and he sat motionless, almost catatonic, for the last two hundred fifty miles of the flight. He also noted a vague and unusual feeling of tightness in his chest. The landing jarred him back into consciousness.

Getting back to his executive office temporarily restored a surge of well-being in him. At least the night security personnel, the only ones still around in the building continued to treat him with deference. He knew he must continue his strategic pursuit of capital for tomorrow's battles, and began to feel the juices flowing again as he dialed up Fred Campion, who a few weeks ago had been so helpful in the financial strangulation of Occidental Healthcare. Mrs. Campion answered the phone.

"Fred is very upset tonight. I'm so glad you called. You know, your TransNational Healthcare was all over the six o'clock news here in California; I'll call him."

"I'm very upset too," Scott remarked, leaning forward into the conversation.

Fred Campion came on the phone, "Richards, how in hell could you let this happen? As a result of our previous conversation, I moved our organization heavily into TransNational Healthcare and when the bottom fell out today we took a bath; my ass is in a real sling."

"Well Fred, that's why I called," Scott lied. "I plan to turn this around. When the dust settles, I'll be in charge of TransNational Healthcare, and you'll be right where you'll want to be. Now here's what we need to do. I need credit."

"Hold it," Fred interrupted. "We unloaded as much of TransNational Healthcare as we could before they closed trading and we aren't going to touch *any* Healthcare stock with a ten-foot pole until things cool off. I'll be lucky if I don't get canned over this. The whole thing looks incredibly unstable. It's a nightmare."

"Now just a minute," Scott was trying to restrain his angst. "All I need from you is some backing, a line of credit, and I can easily turn things around within forty-eight hours, no problem."

"Richards, I never thought you had much of a sense of humor before," Campion said. "That's one of the funniest things I've ever heard in my entire life. I wouldn't, I couldn't, raise a nickel for you, and neither can anyone else in the country. Face it, you're financial poison. I hear you're unemployed, too."

"But—" Scott's reply was cut off by the click of a hang-up followed by the dial tone on the other end. Scott sank into his chair, bathed in sweat. He became acutely aware of a burning in his throat and the center of his chest. He reached for some water, which was in the refrigerator in his credenza wet bar. The pain became a squeezing weight, and he noted with an almost detached mood that the pain was now spreading into his jaw and his breathing was becoming difficult. *Heart attack* leaped into his mind. His instinct told him that this was the real thing, although he somehow felt that he was almost playing a central character in some slow motion, surrealistic drama. He reached the phone receiver with some difficulty and dialed 911.

"Little Rock emergency services," the calm voice came in.

"This is Scott Richards. I'm in the TransNational Tower, top floor and I think I'm having a heart attack." He was getting very short of breath now.

"How can we get to you, sir?"

"Security first floor," Scott was gasping now, since his breathing was much more rapid and labored.

"Is there anyone with you?"

"No, I'm all alone. . . ." The phone receiver started to slip from his hand as his heart rate rose into a swift and irregular rhythm.

"We're on our way. Leave the door open so we can get to you easily." The reassuring voice came over the receiver. Scott had collapsed and was sprawled back in his chair, barely conscious. His eyes focused on the TransNational Healthcare logo, which he had insisted must be embedded in all the glass windows which surrounded his office. It had started to rain and the drops of water made the logo appear to Scott to be melting. This was the last vision he registered before becoming unconscious, the phone receiver silently slipping from his grasp onto the thick carpet. Moments later he didn't hear the dying shrieks of the fire department ambulance as it stopped at the entry hall of the tower. The security guard was incredulous when the paramedics told him where they were going. "We may have a problem getting there because of his protective arrangements," the guard said. "Three elevators and electronic pass cards. Let's go." They started off at a trot. Two minutes and forty-five seconds later, they were at the oak-paneled, steel reinforced door which led to Scott's office. The security guard slipped the last key-card into the slot. "Welcome to TransNational Healthcare Managed Care" came the automated artificial intelligence voice. "Please punch in your special private code on the key pad or push "0" for assistance." The guard was perplexed.

"I don't have a code and there's no one to call for assistance," he told the exasperated medics.

"Blast the door open like they do in cop movies," was their suggestion.

"Well, I don't know . . . okay, I guess."

One reloading and eight-357 Magnum shots later, the door finally yielded. Scott was face down on the floor and the two paramedics rolled him over. Not surprisingly he was without blood pressure, pulse, or respirations. "Triple zero," said the taller of the paramedics.

His shorter partner had already begun cardio-pulmonary resuscitation. He had deftly inserted an intravenous needle into an arm vein and placed an oxygen catheter into the nose of the victim. He then unpacked the battery powered defibrillator. This appeared to the wide-eyed guard to be a very ominous piece of equipment. The electrocardiogram tracing showed an erratic heart rhythm. "We've got V-FIB" he told his colleague.

"Okay, let's do it." And with that statement he brought out of the side of the equipment pack, two round metal discs with long black plastic handles to which coiled electrical cords were attached. He ripped open the hundred and fifty dollar silk shirt, and a grainy paste was liberally spread on Scott's chest and the paddles.

"A hundred joules."

"Okay." Scott's body shuddered as the electric shock was applied.

"Flat line . . . , no, no, now V-Tack."

"Okay, two hundred more."

After a brief resumption of resuscitation, the paddles were again applied and the body convulsed once again as the electrical shock impulse exerted itself. "Hey, we've got sinus rhythm!" exulted the senior operator.

"Pupils still don't respond and God knows what his brain is like," observed his associate.

"Well, let's get him stabilized and into the emergency department. Make sure his Lidocaine drip is going." He turned to the still dazed and incredulous guard. "This guy must have been pretty important, huh?"

"He owned over five hundred hospitals and they say he was worth billions. The hospital where you are going was . . . , ah is, his," answered the security guard.

Ten minutes later, the paramedics wheeled Scott's stretcher through the swinging entry doors of the emergency department at Little Rock-TransNational Healthcare-General (formerly called Little Rock Methodist Medical Center). He explained to the amazed emergency room physician. "We brought your big mogul part-way back, the rest is up to you. We did a great job on his heart, but he was down a long time and I'm not so sure about his brain. He was a triple zero when we got there, and he's still out. Maybe he's just brain-stunned, or maybe he's had it from the neck up. Myocardial infarction, I suppose, 'tho he needs a twelve lead."

The senior paramedic reviewed the resuscitation record with the emergency department triage nurse and the two men then returned to their ambulance ready to respond to the next call. "All in a day's work," the taller paramedic said. "Rich and poor, when we see 'em they all look the same. Some make it, some don't." By this time, the electrocardiogram had confirmed that there was indeed a massive myocardial infarction which was turning Scott's heart muscle into gelatin; his self diagnosis had been correct. The chief of cardiology had been called in and arrived on the scene. "Bad," was his assessment. "Is the cardiac cath center lab up?" he asked the emergency room supervisor.

"We called them as soon as the paramedics radioed in from the field. They're ready," was the reply. At this moment the twenty-eight year old hospital public relations director burst through the curtains surrounding the treatment bay.

"There are already eleven reporters outside looking for a statement," he announced to the assembled medical personnel who unanimously and consistently ignored him as they went about their various professional duties, managing the fluids and medications that now sustained Scott in his state of suspended animation. "What do I tell them?" he persisted. As a journalism-school graduate, he was not used to participating in stressful situations, only in documenting or rationalizing them. The cardiologist finally responded, having decided that it would be easier to swat this gnat than to have him darting around and getting in the way.

"Tell them that Mr. Richards is being admitted for a routine observation, or if you want to, tell them the truth—that he is probably brain dead and we're going to take him to the cardiac-care center where we'll try to get rid of a, probably large, left anterior-descending coronary artery blood clot. That is something that we can probably do, but his brain will still be probably out, maybe permanently. For that, we don't have a treatment. In either case, get out of our way, we're going upstairs."

The media relations director remained in an uncertain and confused state, unclear in his own mind as to how he should deal with a story that, given the day's events, would likely be on all the national wire services within the hour. He chose what he thought was a middle-course. "Mr. Richards has sustained a mild heart attack, but he's in capable hands, the best in the business in one of the premier cardiac centers in the United States, and we anticipate a full and rapid recovery," was his initial optimistic pronouncement.

Scott was wheeled into the sterile environment of the center's cardiac catheterization lab. The doctor, nurses and technicians were already garbed in their robes of surgical gowns and masks, and had the operating table prepared. They quickly threaded a flexible polyethylene life-line up a vein opened in Scott's groin, easing it into his heart. The fixed eye of the fluoroscope recorded each deft movement on tape. When they were positioned to document the site of the problem, a whiff of radio-opaque dye appeared on the X-ray monitor screen.

"Jesus," was the assessment of the lead cardiologist. "We will have to give it a try, but it's gonna be technically tough. This is one of the 1% that separate the men from the boys. Get me the Siemens catheter."

"No can do," said the senior nurse. "We were told they were too costly to replace; we've only got the Harringtons."

"Well, that figures. Mr. Richards will live or die on the basis of that cost-cutting decision." And with that the cardiologist went to work with the tools at hand. When he thought the positioning was proper, he commanded, "Okay, inflate the balloon," referring to the intervention that was supposed to open the clotted blood vessel and restore blood flow to the dead and dying heart muscle. After a pause and a review of the monitor's screen, he ordered again, "Once more, now some dye. Let's see how we're doing." A few more zephyrs of dye went fleeting across the screen. "Damn," he muttered. "We've got a major dissection along the whole vessel. That's always been the problem with those cheap Harringtons."

"We've got V-FIB," interrupted one of the assistant physicians who was assigned to watch the heart rhythm which had become chaotic.

"Not surprised," was the response. "Start with two hundred joules. Everyone stand back."

"Flat line," was the incantation as the monitor now showed no activity.

"EPI," came back the order, and a needle was plunged into the heart and the contents of the attached syringe were injected into the now flaccid ventricle.

"Nothing. Tracing is flat as a pancake," was the voice response which sounded most like a benediction.

"Last ditch calcium," was the concluding suggestion delivered in a resigned tone. Sixty seconds later the EKG monitor screen showed no changes. "Enough. This plus his brain damage makes it easy. We're done, and so is he. Maybe those expensive catheters would look like a better investment now." The cardiologist continued, "Call that yuppie-PR guy, tell him that Scott Richards is dead and he can announce it any way he wants. My suggestion for an epitaph would be *hoisted on his own petard*, or perhaps *on his own catheter.*" With that pronouncement, he went to complete the paperwork on his unsuccessful effort. The nurses were already preparing the body for the morgue. The final common denominator, the toe tag, "Richards, Scott" was attached and the body bag zipped shut. The final act, as the drama came to completion.

CHAPTER 22

Remarkable things happened in the healthcare marketplace the next day, as it seemed the world was turning upside down. Scott's death was prominently recorded, but only as a piece of the crazy twist of events that had overtaken the for-profit health care environment. Ron and Ruth, the new administrative team of TransNational Healthcare were frantically involved in damage control as were many other senior managers in the industry. The law of unintended consequences seemed to be the order of the day. With their stock price plummeting, opportunities to resolve the rapidly multiplying TransNational problems seemed to vanish in rapid sequence. Increasing the level of urgency was the fact that this was a potentially terminal event, a wound for which they now had only a forty-eight hour hiatus to effect a repair, to restore the crumbling enterprise. Crafting a comprehensive coherent solution for a never-ending series of unforeseen problems seemed beyond them. They had started a cascade of events that was now totally out of control. The fact that both American and Occidental Healthcare had declared their previous agreements with TransNational null and void, made the two executives feel even more embattled and with panic all round them, they were, to say the least, stressed and seemingly paralyzed, unable to do any big-picture strategizing. They were unable to orchestrate even any short-term reprieve. Desperation was the prevalent mood of the endless meetings of the senior management group. The panic multiplied, feeding upon itself.

Bill Winter had already sent in his letter of immediate resignation from TransNational and with remarkable hubris had called Charlie Moran to nominate himself as the new Chief Operating Officer of American to "do what was necessary to restore them to efficiency and solvency." Moran thought it over only momentarily. He surmised correctly that Bill could likely soon be under indictment; he'd decided to just accept responsibility and do the job himself. To make matters worse for TransNational Healthcare, the next day's edition of The New York Times printed a suicide letter from Ken Franklin explaining how the current health care financial environment had been such a moral morass for him personally, that he had felt compelled to end his life. It was remarkably well written considering his state of mind at the time, and laid out chapter and verse of how the public had been blinded, as was he, to the rapacious greed of Scott and all those who were manipulating the system to their own financial gain and egregious profits. The paper published all fifteen hundred words and an accompanying editorial put it into historical perspective with the conclusion that "moral dry rot has been ignored for much too long, to the detriment of the health care system, the country and unknown numbers of patients."

The market, in general, had initially been unsure about how best to deal with the rest of the for-profit health conglomerates, although their stock offerings were clearly no longer on anybody's buy list. Ken's letter which subsequently resulted in multiple editorials and stories in print and on television panels and talk shows, became a powerful negative influence on the fate of these entities. Although Occidental Healthcare was able to negotiate temporary bail-out loans, now that the Richards embargo was no longer enforced, the model of investor owned medical consortiums, which had a few days previously dominated the whole industry, was no longer in vogue. It became conventional wisdom for fund managers and advisors who formerly had unabashedly been touting them, to now brand them as pariahs, as they rapidly moved their investors back into computers/electronics and other high-tech stocks. Over the next several weeks, the entire Dow Jones index and NASDAQ fell by fifteen percent. This reflected not only the major global deterioration in the for-profit health care market, but the resultant reverberating ripple effects that went through medical equipment manufacturers, drug companies, and other secondary medical suppliers at this uncertain time as well. "Bears Rampant" was the business headline of the day. Employers who had been happy to do business with TransNational, American, Occidental Healthcare and their clones, for their promises of lower premium costs, suddenly realized that, like their employees, they had been taken advantage of and badly used. The twenty-five percent annual profit margins, the seven and eight-figure salaries and stock option deals of their brothers in senior management of these chains and HMOs were costs that they didn't need to pay. While they were still temporarily contractually locked-in, they were desperately working to seek other options which they were sure must exist or could be developed.

As the entire TransNational Healthcare drama unfolded in public, Dr. Richard White was completing his plan to take advantage of this opportunity. As a physician he had learned early in his career to become comfortable with uncertainty. This skill allowed him to appreciate why he must seize this moment. He'd always been certain something like this would happen to present an occasion for change, but even in his most optimistic dreams had never projected such great possibilities as the current situation presented. Once his thoughts had crystallized, he tracked down Frank Powell and called him at his Texas ranch.

"Mr. Powell," he began. "About that fund you set aside a few years ago, are you game to do something really creative with it?"

"Talk to me," Powell replied. "Thanks to the wonders of compound interest and the fact that we didn't invest any of it in health care stocks, it's up to well over $18 million now."

"Well, it's really quite simple. I want to use it to convene a health care summit, to actually build a program that will function for the benefit of patients. Once we get the process going, I expect that we'll have no problem engaging most of the players. I'd like to use part of your fund to craft and convene a national meeting of health economists, hospital administrators and medical professionals from private, academic, and public sectors. I dare say they've been watching and waiting for an opening such as we're seeing now. I want to call in all our markers and combine multiple talents. I think I can line up the players in short order, if you believe this is how you want the fund to be used."

"I like it; go for it," Powell said. "But remember, it's your fund, not mine. My corporate organization people will provide the support and administrative details. Where do you want to assemble your group?"

"District of Columbia is my first choice. I want the government in early, they need major direction and I think they're going to be receptive to a well thought out plan." As he hung up the phone, Frank Powell was finally a happy man, and for a change was enthusiastically waiting for tomorrow.

Of course, many of Scott's old friends were named as major players in the project. Walter Rand was a co-chair, his socialism had mellowed a little bit, and he now even wore a tie when he delivered his key-note address. Doctor John Armstrong, the former vice-president for medical affairs at TransTexas Healthcare who had resigned when he came to appreciate the ethical and moral flaws in Scott's marketplace-driven plan had become a respected national expert in the clinical development of new ways to provide quality care. Frank Pierce, the former CEO of Coastal Hospital who was now the CEO of a large eastern not-for-profit network, anchored by two prestigious university academic health centers, was another co-chair of the group. Cardinal Riley, now the Pope's representative for New York City, led the deliberations relating to the ethical under-pinnings of the new order of health care. Dean White put himself in charge of plans for research and development. His working group had to determine how to restrain the unlimited use of new and unproven medical technologies while assuring that truly beneficial interventions could reach the clinics and hospitals in short order. This was perhaps the most difficult task of all. Dozens of other experts became involved in these working sessions, which went on for a total of nine weeks. Unlike the Clintons' secretive, lawyer dominated, and ill fated health summit, the players this time were knowledgeable and experienced experts in delivering medical care. The media in Washington had been invited from day one. They soon lost interest, however, since in contrast to the usual political undertakings they covered, endless panels and task force meetings did not make for great headlines. They did, however, make a great blueprint for the transformation of health care, which Congress was only too happy to adopt virtually unchanged in a remarkable show of bipartisanship.

A reinvented national system evolved where private hospitals and physicians carried out the majority of care while the complicated, high technology activities and complex patients went to designated academic settings, where salaried physicians developed and implemented cutting edge treatments. A majority of the research was carried out at these latter sites, with most of the support originating from public funds. The results at these designated sanctuaries were scrutinized and evaluated by expert panels of reviewers who set national standards of excellence for patient care, research directions and outcomes, preventive interventions and educational policies. The whole system went onto a well-established standard fee schedule, and employers simply went to hospitals and doctors' groups to negotiate directly on behalf of their workers, cutting out the profit seeking parties, which had brought the system to its knees in the age of TransNational. Those individual citizens who were under- or uninsured (the number had risen to more than 53 million) had their health insurance premiums paid by government subsidies and Medicare was simply folded into the whole system. In spite of the cost of such programs the budgets balanced, since a 25 percent profit was no longer being taken off the top, and the preventive measures actually became cost effective. There was still competition and decentralization, but quality of care and best medical outcomes became the goal instead of investor profits. The not-for-profit-oriented insurance companies such as Blue Cross had the role of keeping the books, since they already had the information systems to accomplish that job.

Bill Winter was indeed convicted of fraud but after eighteen months in a minimum security facility received a suspended sentence for his activities, cooperating in sorting out the multiple illegal activities at TransNational. He never really totally understood how all of this could have happened simply as a result of his plan; after all, he had only started the process to avenge his sister. As it evolved, however, he had finally subconsciously come to believe that he had somehow been on the side of the angels and all had been for the best. The new catering business that he and his sister Anne had established in Manhattan now seemed exactly the thing that they should be doing, melding her party skills and his accounting management in a family business. Ruth Bonner and Ron George, now Mr. and Mrs. George, had both become born again Christians during their prison terms, and seemed to be very satisfied with their new roles as leading rural religious-social activists in her native Texas working for, of all people, Frank Powell.

By the time a decade had passed, it was clear that the new system really worked and the country and the system got along very well indeed without Scott Richards or his plan.